Unmasked

Unmasked

Jenifer Kanin

ISBN-13: 9781777375508

Table of Contents

Acknowledgements

Special thanks to my family for their inspiration and support

To my editor — Mark Weiler
and
Samantha Brown for the cover art:
samanthabrownstudios.weebly.com
Instagram @twinosha
and
Abigail at New York Book Reviews
For your sage advice and support when I need it most
Check her out on Instagram @newyorkbookreviews
Lastly,
To raccoons, for the many times they have come into my life — for good and for bad.
Follow Gary on Instagram:
@garyunmasked
Email: garyunmasked@gmail.com

CHAPTER 1

Identity

HOW DID IT COME TO this? Everything had changed in an instant. Moments ago, I was full of nothing but power and rage. Now, exhausted, my body wracked with pain, my eyes fixated on the grey mask in my hands as the water ran into the bathroom sink. A part of the mask was now red, soaked in Jenny's innocent blood. A drop of the blood had fallen from the mask and now a bright red stain screamed out to me in contrast to the cold, stark-white sink.

It seemed like a lifetime ago when I first put the mask on. It was more of a joke really than any sort of plan. I thought at worst it might be good for a few laughs — maybe break the boredom for a while — and if it would lead to a few extra benefits for myself, then 'hey, why not?'

It was all Jenny's idea. She was the first one to notice. "You know…. you are the exact same shade of grey as Mrs. Abrams' cat; quite remarkably so!" she mused. "If it were not for the black markings around your eyes and on your tail…." her thoughts trailed off at that point. Jenny often did that, mused about something, trailed off at some point, and that would usually be the end of it. Her mind would jump to the next distraction — the shape of the trees, a new way to get more food from the garden, or how tunnels could be the salvation of everyone in the forest — and off she would go again. She was so full of life and energy, one could not help but be enchanted by her, and would soon try to please her.

That is why I was completely surprised when a few days later she approached me, a strip of steel grey cloth in one hand and paint and a mirror in the other. "Just try it on," she said, "what's the harm?" Whenever she was trying to talk me into something, she would let her long, soft, white ears fall along either side of her head while her pink nose and whiskers twitched with excitement.

My protests didn't seem to slow her down any as she took the cloth into her paws and circled behind me. "Now just close your eyes," she whispered into my ears as she placed the cloth on my face. I could feel her pulling it tight around my eyes, snugging it in the back. *She's putting a blindfold on me? What is this girl up to?* I wondered to myself. "Now open your eyes," she commanded. I expected darkness, nothing but the black that comes from having a blindfold tied around your head. To my surprise, I could see perfectly. If it weren't for the pressure against my face, I would not have known anything was there. "You look perfect!" she said, "in fact, if I didn't know any better, you might even be able to fool me."

"What are you talking about?" I muttered as my mind tried to make sense of her last statement. She interrupted my question by thrusting the mirror into my hand.

"Look for yourself," she said. I have to admit that for a moment, in my confusion, I didn't know what I was looking at. The mask's color was almost a perfect match. You could hardly tell where my fur ended and the fabric began. The image in the mirror — a soft face of all grey fur, with dark intriguing eyes — looked like it belonged to someone else. "Now, we will have to do something about that nose!" Jenny was at it again. "Maybe we can paint it pink."

While she was talking, I just continued to stare into the mirror, occasionally reaching up to feel the mask that was now hiding my own familiar markings. For as long as I could remember, the permanent black mask was a part of me; it defined my face, my identity. 'Trash bandit' is what the locals called me — a villainous creature. Now I could not take my eyes off the reflection of the unfamiliar face looking back at me.

It is a strange and exhilarating feeling to look in the mirror and know that you are looking at yourself, but not recognizing the face in front of you. Once you get over that strange feeling, you start to realize that another feeling is taking its place, the feeling of possibility, of being a different you.

To be honest, it was not the first time my face had taken on an appearance that I did not recognize. I didn't realize it at the time for what it was, but now a familiar feeling washed over me as I stared into that mirror.

"You could be so much more! Why are you wasting your time fooling around with . . . those . . . those . . . ANIMALS!" my mother's shrill screams rang in my ears. I rushed into the bathroom to escape her wrath. I was at the point of my life that some might call a teenage rebellion. Not that I was any kind of a rebel. Most of my childhood was spent quietly alone, not really being noticed by anyone. Even in my own family, I was overshadowed by the drama of my siblings. I would spend much of my time by myself, wandering in the woods or playing by the creek. Looking back on it now, I wonder if anyone even noticed that I was not around.

As I got older, I started to test the expectations of my parents and others in an attempt to change how people perceive me. I started hanging around some of the older kids in the area. At first, my mother did not notice. She just seemed happy that I had made some friends and was out of the house.

Then we started getting into trouble. At first, it was just stupid stuff, like knocking over the trash cans on the street or leaving little 'presents' in the Tylers' swimming pool. As is often the case in life, every action eventually brings about a reaction. The Tyler's started letting out their Rottweiler to protect the neighborhood from the mischievous creatures that roamed the streets after sundown.

The night in question that had pushed my mom over the edge, we had once again been up to no good, prowling the streets to see what kind of trouble we could get into. Little did we know, the hound was waiting for us. When he charged, it was 'every creature for himself', and we all scrambled in different directions to escape the salivating jaws bearing down on us.

Just my luck, it seemed to be my scent that the beast had locked on to. I had just started to clamber up the nearest tree when the dog leaped up into the air and caught the tip of my tail. I winced from the searing pain but managed to dig my claws into the bark and hold on for dear life. Fortunately, all he got was an unsatisfying mouthful of fur. Once the carnivorous canine crashed back to the earth, I saw my opportunity and managed to climb further up the tree to safety. Now out of reach of the Rottweiler — who was still furiously hurling himself against the trunk of the tree — I stared down at him for a moment and contemplated how close I had come to an inglorious end.

As soon as I entered our home, my mother took one look at my general appearance and mutilated tail tip and started screeching. That was when I took refuge in the bathroom. Splashing cold water on my face I looked into the mirror. There it was. For just one instant, I did not recognize myself. The image reflecting back at me was disconnected from the person I thought I was. It was not that my face was different, but it was *I* that was different.

Thinking about it now, I realize I was seeing the choices I was making and who those choices were leading me to become. Looking into that mirror, with the sound of my mother's cries in the background and a throbbing feeling in my tail, I was forced to confront the questions: *Is this really who I am? Who I want to be?*

It was not the only time the face in the mirror would make me wonder who I was. As I got older, I started to notice that the image I saw each day reflected in the mirror started to change. It was as if the mirror kept score of every wrong choice and missed opportunity in my life. You start to see the expectations and disappointments that build up day after day, year after year, over the course of a lifetime. These build with each passing day, with each failure or success, with each decision and choice that you make. Slowly, over time, life's scorecard was being filled out on the image in the mirror.

But now, in this moment in my life, as I gazed into the mirror Jenny gave me, a feeling of excitement was building; a sort of liberation started to set in. *If the image before me is me, but not me . . . then whose image is it? Who am I looking at? This person could be anyone. This face has failed at nothing; disappointed no one. This face is only potential, only promise.*

Jenny's voice brought me back to the moment. "Yes, a little dab of pink on the nose, I have just the thing!" She bounded off behind the bushes. A few seconds later she emerged with a ripe strawberry. "Hold still," she said as she smushed the strawberry into my nose. "Now you will have to resist the urge to wipe it off, and it is a bit redder than pink, but it will have to do!" Her statement held with it a certain sense of self-satisfaction. "The old woman's eyesight is not the best anyways, so for now, it will have to do. Now off you go. See if you can pull it off!" I detected a slight giggle in Jenny's voice as she pushed me toward the house.

"Off I go? Where am I going?" My feet were backpedaling but I couldn't help but notice that I was still moving forward.

"Why, off to see if you can impersonate the cat of course," Jenny said with a wry smile, her pale blue eyes looking at me coyly, as only a bunny can. "While you are at it see what you can rummage up for us to eat!"

Now the Abrams farm had long been a legend to the animals in the forest. Stories of abundant food and warmth were known by everyone who lived in the valley and the hills surrounding the place. On cold winter nights, when food was scarce to find, tales were told to the children of a bounteous table filled with every delicious thing imaginable. As little ones, we loved to name our favorite foods and ask if they were there on the table. "Mama, was there fish there?" I would ask.

"Yes dear, many of the finest oily fishes," Mama would reply.

"Mama, was there cake there?" my sister would inquire.

"Oh yes, the finest of cakes, still warm from the oven," would be Mama's answer.

We would fall asleep dreaming of all the yummy morsels that the house contained. These stories had been passed on to many down through the generations. Occasionally some incredible morsel would be found by someone who was brave enough to explore close to the farm and the surrounding buildings. This just added to the legend.

The cat door was a particularly tempting target. We had been watching it since we were children. It was the access point between our world and theirs. When it swung open, it emitted light and heat that was a source of fascination to all of us. The warm air that wafted outwards always seemed to carry a scent of sweetness. *Was that bread? Meat?* The alluring aroma changed every time the door swung open.

For all its temptations, another emotion always kept us from getting too close or trying to enter the swinging door — fear. Any who dared to approach the door were quickly overwhelmed with a sense of dread. It had become a sort of game to us. We would sneak up to the home and then dare someone to go inside. Most of us would approach the door, only to turn and run away once we got within a couple of feet. Johnny was the only one of us who was brave enough to make a serious attempt. I remember the night he swore that he would get inside and find out what was on the other side.

His approach to the house was flawless, using all the cunning and caution that opossums were known for. No sound was heard in his step; no shadow cast where he didn't want it. Alongside the wall he crept. When he reached the side door, the night was still and completely silent.

He made his move to open the door, and then everything soon fell apart. The first push of his paw brought no response. The door simply flapped — in, out, in, out. He waited a few moments and then made his move to enter the house. It was when he started to push his face into the door that everything changed. I can still hear the sound if I close my eyes — a deep and terrifying sound. Johnny had gotten his body about halfway into the house...

His screams send shivers up my spine even now. I am not sure what was happening inside the house, but from the outside we could hear the piercing cries of someone in intense pain. It was obvious that something had grabbed him from the other side. Johnny's hind feet were doing everything they could to pull him back out of the door and away from the house, yet no matter how hard he struggled, he couldn't shake himself free. The low guttural sounds — combined with Johnny's screams of terror — filled the night.

We all thought that was the end of Johnny, but in the commotion, he somehow managed to pull himself free. The half that emerged from the house was barely recognizable. His fur was soaking wet and matted; blood was streaming down his face. Even from the bushes, we could hear the sound of a great beast hurling himself against the door, furiously clawing and scratching in a desperate attempt to break down the barrier. With each powerful impact, we felt the vibrations pulsate through our bodies as the creature, in his madness, relentlessly tried to break out and finish what it had started.

Johnny stumbled as he backed his broken body away from the house towards the leafy undergrowth nearby where we were watching. Stunned by the recent events, it took a moment for us to recover and rush to his aid. His body lay broken and defeated before us. None of us thought he was going to make it, and — in a way — the Johnny we knew didn't.

And now she wants me to go near this place? In the daytime? Is she crazier than a nine-legged spider? "One more thing," Jenny laughed a little as she spoke, and I knew I wasn't going to like what she said next, "you will need to change the way you walk a little."

"What's wrong with the way I walk?" I protested. The comment distracted me enough that my feelings of self-consciousness made me forget the imminent danger.

"It's not very graceful. You kind of hunch over and skulk around like you're walking on hot sand at the beach all the time. You need to lengthen your stride and glide as you walk, and try not to arch your back so much — if you can!"

There was a note of challenge in Jenny's voice that made me want to prove her wrong. "Like this?" I said, more of a question than I wanted it to be.

"No, your back still doesn't look right. My god, it is like you are part camel with that thing." I gave it a second try, thrusting my stomach towards the ground in what felt like a poor impression of a raccoon doing yoga. "Yeah, now you're getting it . . . that's starting to look right . . . only, the tail is off. Yours is pointing down all the time, dragging on the ground. Does it have to do that?" She said it so sweetly that, for the moment, the urge to please her outweighed the feeling that I had just been insulted.

"No, I can move it," and I started to wag my tail back and forth.

"Cute, but the wrong animal. Can you point it straight behind you? Or straight up in the air?"

I gave another pass in front of Jenny — my tail straight out behind me — doing my best to gracefully 'glide' all the while thrusting my stomach in such a way that my back was parallel to the ground. Jenny let out a gleeful giggle like she does when one of her crazy plans starts to come together. "Now try it with the tail straight up in the air and quicken your pace a little like you are excited to see someone." I circled around again and headed straight to Jenny. It was a strange sensation to have my tail up like that. A little wind gust reminded me that I was more exposed than I was used to. "That's perfect!" she cried, "I think you're ready. We need to do a test run! Follow me!" She quickly bounded through the bushes towards the south side of the Abrams house. The human that lived there kept a vegetable garden that we liked to visit when no one was looking. The garden was full of every delicious thing you could imagine, and it was a constant battle between us trying to get in, and Mrs. Abrams trying to keep us out. Many years ago, Mr. Abrams had built a stone wall around the garden in an attempt to secure the produce from our ancestors, not that it kept any of us out. But we understood its purpose and tried to be a little more discreet when we did our shopping, lest some more effective countermeasures be put into place.

"The old woman is always out in the garden this time of day," Jenny called back to me as she neared the back corner of the Abrams property.

The location was sheltered nicely by some large blackberry bushes. The thicket of canes would block the view of anyone looking down in our direction, but it provided us with a good enough view to see what was happening in the garden. "There she is," Jenny lowered her voice even though we were far enough away that no one could hear us. "If this is ever going to work, now is the time to find out. See, it looks like she even left the gate unlatched. You just have to give it a good push and you should be able to walk right in."

"Walk right in? Are you mad Jenny? Why would I want to do that?" The confused look on my face made it obvious to Jenny that I had missed the main point of her master plan.

"To see if you can fool the old lady into thinking that you are the cat. Just think of the possibilities!" I was having a hard time thinking of the possibilities when she added: "Remember you are still wearing the mask."

I had completely forgotten about the mask. It felt like hours ago that Jenny had put it around my head. Now it seemed like it had always been a part of me. So much so that I had to reach up and touch my face to see if it was still there. The simple act of touching the mask reminded me of the possibility that I could choose to become anyone that I wanted to be. It stirred within me a feeling of confidence that I didn't expect.

My newfound boldness quickly evaporated when my very next thought was the image of Mrs. Abrams' big boot impacting my ribs with the force of a kicking mule. Having second thoughts and rubbing my side in a sort of sympathy for events yet to unfold, I protested, "There is no way that this will work Jenny."

She looked at me with her large, pale blue eyes. "Just give it a try. Please? I know this will work! Her eyesight is not that good, and everything will be okay if you just remember the things that we practiced. I know you can do it!"

She sounded so convincing, even I was starting to believe her. "Okay, but what if it doesn't work? What then?" I tried to sound brave but pragmatic.

"If it doesn't work you will know right away. She will tense up or scream or something. If that happens, just use that mighty hump of yours to run to the apple tree in the corner. From there you can climb over the garden wall and out to safety on that branch there," she pointed to a branch that had grown out beyond the northeast corner of the garden, "and then drop down outside the wall. In all the confusion, you can make it back to the bushes behind the house. What is the worst that can happen?"

What's the worst that can happen? I started imaging a long list of the worst things that could happen, Mrs. Abrams' boot once again rising to the top of the list. *Wait a minute, did she say mighty hump?* Jenny quickly leaned in and touched her nose to mine before I could come up with a witty retort to her painfully accurate description of me. She dabbed my nose again with a strawberry in a transparent attempt to distract me from my own indignation. "Just remember all the things we practiced, the walking, the vocalizations — just *be* the cat. If it doesn't work, I prom- ise I will make it up to you". With that, Jenny gave me a gentle shove out of the brambles and I reluctantly turned and started walking cautiously towards the unlatched gate.

Be the cat. Be the cat. Jenny's words became my mantra as I made my way to the garden's entrance. While I was in the process of convincing my mind of who I was, my body was in the act of trying its best to prove otherwise. As I made the first few steps through the grass, it was as if I had forgot- ten how to control my limbs. I had to consciously think about every step, instead of just doing something I had done every day of my life up to that point without really even noticing. Funny how hard it is to change the simplest thing once the pattern has become ingrained. If I remembered the walk, I forgot the tail. If I remembered the tail, my back would return to its — let's say — elegant curve. Lucky for me, Mrs. Abrams was bent over in the garden and unaware of my clumsy approach. By the time I reached the gate, I had managed to coordinate my movements enough to do a passable impression of a cat, if not *the* cat. I gave one last glance over my shoulder to where Jenny was waiting in the blackberry bushes, took a deep breath, and pushed my way through the gate.

CHAPTER 2
The Perplexing Possums

"WHAT ARE WE LOOKING AT?" Max was not a stranger to investigating unusual happenings. He had a nose for trouble and could never resist the mental exercise of solving a good mystery. Problems had a way of finding him anyway, so he decided he might as well embrace the role.

Max had a personality that people trusted; steady, reliable, never panicking in a crisis. He could very well have been the inspiration for the expression "smart as a fox". You could see it whenever he was investigating something. He had a way of lowering his head and absorbing all the information that could be taken in. Dark brown, intelligent eyes would survey the scene. His large ears would rarely miss a sound. A keen sense of smell would root out any clues left behind. Although being a fox did not automatically mean that you were intelligent. Max had a cousin whose favorite pastime was having the other animals watch to see how many pinecones he could shove up his nose in sixty seconds. The answer usually turned out to be two, with fifty-eight awkward seconds to follow. You would think that if he had any sense, he would at least pick something small like blueberries. At least then some suspense would be created with each new attempt.

"The whole family appears to have just disappeared," Jonathan replied. "The neighbor says she saw them all leave after sunset to go foraging like they do every night. Nothing out of the ordinary. That was over a week ago. She hasn't seen them since." Jonathan was a good assistant — straight to the facts without getting lost in the details. Of course, chipmunks are just wired that way — direct and to the point. When you are small, distractions tend to have dangerous consequences. Jonathan added to his directness a level of focus that most others of his kind were lacking.

Max entered the den to take a look around. Everything seemed perfectly normal. The home was a common design for possums. The large central tunnel had various rooms and passageways dug into the sides, heading off in different directions like the branches of a tree. There was a bedroom through the first tunnel on the right; a kitchen and dining area through the next tunnel on the left; a series of smaller passageways forked out from the end of the shaft to the family's sleeping areas. Modest to be sure but someone put their heart into the digging.

Max entered the bedroom to see if there was anything that could provide a clue to the current location of the family. If there was going to be any evidence that the family left of their own choosing, it would be in there. He picked up a picture from off the dresser. Mom, Dad, and a half dozen possum children were smiling with a nice babbling brook in the background. It looked like a family vacation. *Maybe they decided to go back?* The bitter feeling in the pit of his stomach told him otherwise.

Looking around the home, all of the items you would expect to be taken if you were packing for a trip were still in their proper place. Dresser drawers were full of clothing. Brushes and personal items were in their containers on the bathroom sink. There was no evidence that anyone packed for a trip or was planning to leave for an extended period of time. It looked like they just disappeared and left everything behind.

Max went into the kitchen to look for any other clues; a calendar on the fridge or even a Post-it note that would indicate that the family was planning on being away for a while. "Nothing in the children's rooms or the bathrooms. Everything looks like they should all be returning any moment," Jonathan chirped. "I can't find anything to suggest they went away or were even planning to leave." Max opened the fridge and helped himself to a beer. "What are you doing?" asked Jonathan "We just can't start taking their stuff!"

"I have a feeling they won't be needing it anymore," Max said in a tone that made Jonathan stop looking around. It had a sense of finality, and Jonathan knew that Max had already drawn his conclusion. "Come on," Max said, "there's nothing more to learn here. Let's go back outside and see if we can find anyone that saw them after they left home."

CHAPTER 3

Eleanor Place

ELEANOR PLACE WAS THE KIND of street that people wanted to move to when they were ready to start a family. Nestled in a quiet part of a bustling city, the street could easily have fit into a scenic alpine village. The area's geographical features are what made it unique. Most houses either backed on to a ravine to the east or were tucked up against the rocky hillside to the west. This meant that instead of the usual neighborhood with row after row of housing, Rocky Pines was a quiet community with just a few streets and houses tucked in wherever nature allowed.

Eleanor Place could be found at the southernmost point of Rocky Pines. The area was filled with stately trees, untouched for at least a century or two. Towering white pines filled the hillside and extended down into the ravine amongst the rocks to give the area its name. The street ended in a cul-de-sac as the ravine curved in front of its path, as if a great finger from the sky gouged a line in the earth to say: 'this far and no further'.

The homes in the area were added slowly over the decades, so you got a little bit of everything. A turn of the century brick Victorian could easily be found next one of many smaller war time homes that were being bought up and replaced by larger modern dwellings. It was a trend that was increasing as home prices in the city continued to climb. A variety of other homes built in the seventies and eighties only added to the area's contrast of architecture styles.

Eleanor Place reflected all these trends. At the very end of the cul-de-sac stood Mrs. Abrams' red brick Victorian. It showed its age and was noticeably the first house built in the area. Just looking at it, you could easily picture it sitting there all by itself — a narrow dirt road leading up to it — filled with a large family that thought of themselves as living out in the wilderness, well outside the city limits. The property was quite deep, and it was hard to tell where it ended as it fell away with the steep sides of the ravine. The lush garden in the back of the home soaked up the southern sun, a rich reward to the builders of the home that had the sense to clear enough of the trees behind the house to create one of the neighborhood's few open, sunny spaces.

To the right of Mrs. Abrams' place was a small bungalow where Mr. and Mrs. Williams lived. They were both in their seventies but were the kind of people that swore they would never leave. "Nobody will ever put me into a nursing home! Lousy places where they hide old people away to wait for them to die!" Mr. Williams used to say whenever anyone would give him the chance. "I'll die right here on my kitchen floor if I have my way . . . " he would usually catch himself at this point, the mental image of being helpless on the floor and no one hearing him would be enough to get him on to another topic. They had three adult children — one boy, the oldest, and two girls — that would come to visit from time to time. The girls were nice enough and would busy themselves with cleaning up and helping around the house when they came to visit.

The son was the sort that gave you the feeling he was in a bad mood all the time. He could frequently be heard telling them that they are 'too old to be living out here anymore,' and 'why do you think you can still keep up with the maintenance on this old place?' Instead of loving concern for his aged parents, it was dollar signs that could be seen in his eyes as he looked around the area at the new homes going in and envisioned selling their large property to someone that would tear the place down to build another expensive home in the area.

Next to the Williams were Ethan and Felicity Jackson. Their pie-shaped lot was the last house on the west side of the street. The rocky outcrop to their north made it impossible to build another house beside them. It was not until the street bent around the rocks that another house would appear on the west side of Eleanor Place. The Jackson home was a lovely ranch style that took advantage of the long wide lot it was built upon.

Felicity Jackson was the classic Stepford wife. She was devoted to her home and children and perky in a way that bordered on annoying. She could flash you a look that would almost dare you to be angry with her, and in the next moment smile so sweetly that most people would let her have what she wanted. As a girl, she had learned that being beautiful meant that most of the things she thought she wanted were easily accessible to her. But that advantage did not come without its price. The smile on her face became more of a reflex, rather than a reflection of her genuine emotions.

Her husband Ethan worked long hours as a computer programmer, which left the child rearing and housework to his wife. They were blessed with two children. The firstborn — Thomas, aged 10 — liked cars and computers and anything that would annoy his mother. Emily was 6 and could have been plucked from the pages of a magazine. She had bright, blue eyes with curly, blonde hair. The greater part of Felicity's day was consumed with trying to create the perfect picture which would subsequently be shared with the rest of the world. On occasion she might have wondered if she was truly happy, but to allow such a worrying thought would have risked ruining her image.

To the left of Mrs. Abrams' property lived the Asters. Theirs was a stunning property with a large yard and a view of the ravine. They were both in their sixties and it was obvious that they had money. Mr. Aster had worked in finance, and a few well-timed investments paid to demolish two smaller houses and construct the current tribute to glass and stone they called home. They never had children, with the exception of their two prize-winning grey Skye terriers — Mitzy and Lulu Belle. These were afforded the affection normally reserved for a child.

John and Elizabeth Sampson lived next to the Asters in a nice split-level home. At the time it was built, it was one of the nicest homes in the area. Now it appeared a bit outdated and in need of a few repairs. John had received a few offers to buy the place, but he viewed himself as a simple man, content to leave things the way they were and not be fussing about, trying to get ahead. The Sampsons had three children. Two of them were now teenagers with driver's licenses and were out more than they were in.

The two older children had spent most of their childhood scrambling down the hill behind the house to get to the creek at the bottom of the ravine. Elizabeth Sampson spent the better part of the last decade yelling down the hill for the children to come back home. *Lord knows they could catch their death down there.*

The third child was a late surprise. Just when John and Elizabeth thought they could see the light at the end of the tunnel in that their children were nearly grown and independent, nature had other plans. At first, John thought that Becky's symptoms could be explained by some near-to-the-expiry-date ham the family had consumed a few days before. Nothing could prepare him for the shock that her symptoms were from another kind of little ham in the belly; confirmed by a pregnancy test a few weeks later. A little less than nine months later they were starting the adventure of raising a child all over again, this time a little wiser, but lacking some of the energy they had when their firstborn had arrived.

CHAPTER 4

Success in the Garden

THE GATE TO THE GARDEN opened easier than I thought it would. As I pushed it, it swung wide open and I felt like I was a notorious outlaw bursting through the doors of the only saloon in town, ready to draw against anyone who crossed my path. I paused for a moment before I entered, a little out of caution, a little for dramatic effect. In reality, my entry to the garden went largely unnoticed, and Mrs. Abrams did not even look in my direction, she just continued in the unending labor of pulling weeds from the vegetable garden.

My instincts were telling me to try and avoid direct contact with humans at all costs, that nothing good could come from being anywhere near them, so I started to shuffle along the brick wall inside of the garden in the opposite direction of Mrs. Abrams. I had almost made it to the corner of the brick wall, when my reason caught up with my impulses and the thought dawned on me that there was not much point to a stealth approach. *What is the point of the mask and disguise if not to be seen?* I thought to myself while at the same time noticing how well Mrs. Abrams' crop of rutabagas was coming in. *If something went wrong, I could be up the apple tree and out of the garden basking in Jenny's praise and admiration before the old lady knew what was happening.* At least the plan sounded reasonable inside my head and I regained a measure of confidence. I also came to the conclusion that the real benefit of the direct approach would be to bring this whole charade to a conclusion quickly, one way or another.

I did a quick about-face and started walking directly towards Mrs. Abrams. I had resigned myself to the fact that an old lady's stiff boot to my side was the most probable outcome in my immediate future, and I might as well get it over with. At least I could milk it for a few days of attention from Jenny trying to put things right. *What was I thinking Gary? Here, let me get that for you!* Thinking of Jenny fawning over me brought a smile to my face, partially due to the thought of being the recipient of her attention, but also because in the scene playing out in my mind, my Jenny impersonation was spot on. *Let me rub your side for you — you big brave raccoon — how could I get such a crazy idea in my head? And you were sooooo brave!* Jenny's imagined platitudes had distracted me to the point that I almost daydreamed myself into a collision with Mrs. Abrams. I came to a sudden stop about an ear of corn's length away from her.

Not sure of what to do I sat myself down on my hind legs. What was it Jenny tried to teach me to say? "Reow!" spewed out of my lips . . . no that didn't sound right . . . "Beow". It was a good thing Mrs. Abrams was losing her hearing as well as her eyesight. "Is that you Mr. Pickles?" Mrs. Abrams called out; her voice crackled with her age.

"Meow," I replied. *Think I got it that time.* Mrs. Abrams stopped what she was doing and turned towards me. A slow-motion *"ooohhh nooooo . . ."* started to play in my mind but the next thing I knew she was patting me on the head and telling me what a good kitty I was. Mrs. Abrams' hand on my head — stroking the side of my face, with a little scratch to my chin — felt better than anything I had experienced before. "Meow!" just seemed to come out of me as I rubbed up against Mrs. Abrams and present my backside to her. A few scratches at the base of my tail and I almost forgot why I was there.

"That's a good kitty, Mr. Pickles. Now I have to be getting back to my weeding."

The whole plan was progressing flawlessly when Mrs. Abrams' petting of my back started to slow down. "Why Mr. Pickles," she said, "your fur feels rougher and coarser than usual." My heart started to sink. *Is this it? Is this the end? Did she realize what a fraud I am?* "You must have been rolling in something! We will have to give you a nice warm bath tonight! Now run along I have more work to do in my garden."

I took that as my cue to leave and turned to start heading back to the gate. My mind was whirling with the recent events and I had more questions than answers. *Did she really believe I was the cat? Why did it feel so good when she was stroking me? I am the world's greatest impersonator? What else could I do with this power?* I had allowed myself to fantasize about the many things I could eat from the garden with full access and no fear of reprisal from Mrs. Abrams. My dreams of a belly full of fresh, ripe berries came to an abrupt end when I arrived at the garden gate.

CHAPTER 5

Mr. Pickles

MAKE NO MISTAKE; A CAT'S life is a pretty good life. If you were to boil down everything you wanted from this world, what would it be? To be unconditionally loved and cared for? To have food provided for you whenever you needed or desired? To hear constant praise and reassurances that you are good and that you are wanted? To feel the warm touch of those you love upon you as you drift in and out of 12 to 14 hours of sleep every day?

Such was the life of Mr. Pickles. From the time that he was a kitten, Mrs. Abrams spoiled him. The Abrams children had long ago moved away, busy with families of their own, far from their ancestral home on Eleanor Place. Mr. Abrams had died of a heart attack more than a decade ago, and that left Mrs. Abigail Abrams — elderly and alone — caring for the farm that she spent her entire adult life on. After decades of being absorbed in the familiar routine of caring for husband and family, Mr. Pickles was now the only one left for her to love and care for, and he would be the recipient of all that attention. Such was the glorious life of Mr. Pickles.

The good life had taken its toll on Pickles. Instead of being the nocturnal hunting machine that he had been in his youth, it was all too easy to spend the night curled up with Mrs. Abrams, absorbing all the body heat she could provide. Mrs. Abrams never got used to cooking for one, so that meant a constant oversupply of tasty delights coming out from her kitchen. You would not think pies and pastries would be the usual diet for a cat, but put enough butter in anything and even a ferocious feline will quickly develop a taste for it. In his youth, Pickles was as sleek as a serpent and as stealthy as a panther at midnight. Lately, he had noticed it was getting more and more difficult to squeeze thought the cat door. He found himself far too frequently having to inhale and hold his breath just make the egress outside for the night. Still, Pickles saw himself as he once was, a mighty hunter; quick like a fox; to be feared by all. It was this Mr. Pickles that noticed someone coming out of the garden and towards the garden gate — *his* garden gate.

CHAPTER 6

Confrontation in the Garden

Seeing Mr. Pickles waiting for me at the entrance to the garden brought everything back into focus. I was a raccoon impersonating a cat, the very same cat that was now blocking my exit. In an attempt to calm myself, I remembered how Mrs. Abrams was completely fooled by my appearance.

Mr. Pickles, on the other hand, had no problem seeing through my disguise. The fur on his back stood straight up and he started to utter this low ungodly sound — "merrrrroooowwwww". It was the type of sound that was meant to set your nerves on edge, and I had to admit, it was remarkably effective at the moment. On the plus side, this was a sound I had never heard a cat make before, and my brain made a note to file that away somewhere for future use. At least part of my brain believed I would be alive long enough to be able to use it. *Foolish brain.*

My choices were clear. Turn tail and run, giving up all hope of the illusion that I was Mr. Pickles, or double down on the bluff and confront the situation. Maybe an opportunity to escape would present itself later.

"Mmmmerrowww," I growled — going all in — trying my best to imitate the sound that Mr. Pickles had just made. Cat-on-cat battle here we come. "Merrrrroooowwwww," Mr. Pickle replied, somehow it was much more intimidating coming from him.

"Mmm mmm eeer oooow?" *Could a cat ask a question and stutter at the same time?* I seemed to have found a way. Mr. Pickles started to crouch down with his hind legs slightly elevated, and with his rear end wiggling slightly and his tail whipping back and forth. He was getting ready to spring into action, turning this war of words into a full-on catfight.

Just as I was preparing for the worst — wondering how a raccoon would fare fending off 15 pounds of teeth and claws (okay maybe 20 pounds taking into account Mr. Pickles' pastry rounded physique) — Mrs. Abrams came to an unlikely rescue. "Get away you mangy stray!" she cried swinging her shovel at Mr. Pickles. "Go back to where you came from!" The old lady was trying her best to whack the intruder on his melon with her spade. Mr. Pickles, confused by the sudden turn of events and seeing the source of his delicacies turn against him, quickly bid a hasty retreat to the hydrangea bushes near the back door of the house.

I, on the other hand, felt a rush of relief and euphoria wash over me. Not only was I safe from Mr. Pickles, but I was also now armed with the knowledge that Mrs. Abrams chose to protect me over her real cat. *Maybe I could pull this off.*

I strutted out of the garden with all the confidence of a lion, both feline and regal, heading back to the woods to revel in Jenny's praise. That is when I came to a second realization. Not only had I out-impersonated Mr. Pickles at being himself, but the authentic albeit humiliated Mr. Pickles had another surprise coming. A long, hot, soapy bath, courtesy of yours truly, was in his immediate future.

CHAPTER 7

Clueless

MAX AND JONATHAN COMPLETED THEIR search of the area outside the home. They could find no evidence of digging or that something had disturbed the soil around the entrance. There were no unusual tracks or patterns to indicate something might have snuck in to make a meal for themselves. If anything, everything was a little too clean for Max, like when you were a kid and your parents would come home to find the house immaculate. The parents' first instinct is not to say 'my, what great kids we have!' It is to suspiciously wonder what happened that made the kids have to clean up, and what were they trying to hide? Everything around the home was tidy in a way that made Max wonder if someone had covered their tracks.

The next logical step was to start interviewing everyone who lived in close proximity to the possum residence. Working out in concentric circles from the home, Max and Jonathan determined to speak to everyone they could and see if they could cause some ripples. Max's keen fox senses meant he would take the ground animals like the frogs and the mice, all the while seeing if he could sniff out clues. That left the birds and tree-dwelling animals to the more vertically nimble Jonathan. One of the benefits of being a chipmunk is the ability to almost defy the law of gravity.

Everyone they spoke to told a similar story. No, they had not seen the family for days, and no, they had no idea where they could be. The family was well-liked by all the creatures that lived around them. As omnivores that were not known to do much killing — other than grubs and worms — they had very little competition with the neighbors and few enemies. The squirrels told of how the family would sometimes share with them the extra nuts they had gathered. A gopher told of a night when he had been chased by the Asters' terriers Mitzy and Lulu, and if it were not for the possums giving him shelter in the burrow, he would have been done for. The possum family was known to move about from time to time, but anyone who knew them thought it was odd that they would leave their belongings behind, and that they would not tell anyone that they were leaving.

CHAPTER 8

The Asters

MR. AND MRS. CLAUDE AND Julia Aster were enjoying their early retirement immensely. They were well known in the arts community with Julia Aster being a magnanimous supporter of the local theater scene. They were always at the premieres of anything important, despite the long drive into the city's downtown core, and Mrs. Aster loved to see and be seen by the society crowd. Mr. Aster would have been content to stay at home with a good book and a glass of expensive single malt, reading in front of the fireplace. But theater was important to Julia and it is never a bad thing to have a happy wife.

They had no children, but it was not for a lack of trying. Mrs. Aster spent years going to fertility specialists and outlaid a small fortune on therapies and treatments. In the end, nothing that she tried was effective and her wish to be pregnant and have a baby was not to be. The Asters went through a difficult time in their marriage when they came to the inevitable realization that they were not going to be able to have children and then had to deal with their disappointment and the finality of their loss; any remaining flicker of hope had been permanently extinguished. Mrs. Aster went from sorrow to anger, and then from anger to blaming herself for their loss. In an act of self-preservation, her blame turned outward toward her husband and to the idea that somehow, and in some way, it must be his fault. Her guilt at carrying such unsubstantiated resentment towards her husband led her back to feeling guilty about herself. She spiraled down into a deep depression from which she could not escape, convinced that her husband would eventually leave her for a younger woman that could bear him a plethora of children.

As happens when a loved one is plunged into a dark, internal battle, Mr. Aster, while aware that his wife was struggling, was at a loss as to how to help her. He would try and reassure her that he loved her, but somehow the timing was always a little bit off. Or the effort would not bear fruit because of one or two misplaced words that would send his wife crashing into despair, feeling criticized and misunderstood, no matter how comforting his preceding words had been. He started to make the same mistake that many husbands do, figuring it was better to leave Julia alone rather than make her more upset unintentionally.

The Asters almost did not make it through those rough years. Mr. Aster buried himself in work and found a way to be gone most of the time. Mrs. Aster would hardly leave the house, consumed by her depression and sorrow. They were both at the point where they were wondering if this was the end of their marriage.

The path out of the darkness started with a single night and a single conversation on an unseasonably cool November night. It was one of those rare days when Julia had been feeling well enough to go out to the grocery store and pick up a few things for dinner. Mr. Aster found himself alone at home that evening. The sun had started to set, and the temperature was dropping, so he started a fire in the fireplace. As the flames started to consume the wood and the smoke began to rise, he found himself in good spirits. *Something primal about a fire,* he thought to himself as his gaze fixed upon the dancing flames.

It was then that he saw the old photo albums on the shelf next to the fireplace. He took one out and started flipping through the pages. Old pictures of himself and Julia, from a time before they had gotten married.

We were so young! The thought kept running through his mind as he turned the pages. Pictures showed Julia laughing and smiling; he had almost forgotten how vibrant and beautiful she was then. All the memories of their happier times together and how in love they were crashed over him in wave after wave of emotion.

In a stroke of good timing that probably saved their marriage, Julia arrived home from her grocery shopping. Going out for the first time in a few days had lifted her mood and she entered the home to find her husband on the living room floor in front of the fireplace with the family photo albums spread out around him. She could immediately sense his emotions and noticed a single tear streaming down her husband's face. When their eyes met, she immediately burst into tears, though not fully sure of the reason why.

They spent the evening right there on the floor with a bottle of wine, reminiscing about the moments in time that the old photos had captured. The pictures brought back so many good memories and feelings. It was in that state of mind, that for the first time in a long time, they both were able to share how they had been feeling without judgment or blame. That is not to say that all their problems were solved in one night. It was a little more like blowing on some smoldering embers. The coals start to glow again and eventually a small flame can appear. It is a beginning that can be built upon, but quickly needs small acts of love and kindness stacked upon it, to burn in any meaningful or lasting way.

One of those small acts of kindness was the day that Mr. Aster came home with a banker's box tied with a big red bow. He made Julia sit down on the sofa and close her eyes before he would give her the surprise. "What do you think it is?" he asked.

"Well, a box of that size looks like it could hold eight to ten reams of paper. Did you get me printer paper you romantic devil?" she giggled a little as she teased him. It was nice to see her sense of humor coming out again.

The suspense was broken by the sound of scratching inside the box. Julia opened her eyes wide, "it's alive?" she asked in wondering disbelief. As soon as the words were out of her mouth the lid of the box popped open to reveal two tiny, furry, grey Skye Terriers looking back at her. It was love at first sight for all three of them. The soon to be named Mitzy and Lulu Belle were about to embark on a life of luxury and bask in what a woman with a large disposable income could shower upon them.

CHAPTER 9

Childhood

LET ME TELL YOU A little about my family. I was raised in a large oak tree that had gradually ascended out of the ravine floor for hundreds of years. The tree was majestic, with the main trunk so thick, a grown man could not reach his arms even half-way around it. The branches spiraled out from the trunk's main axis, weaving their way among the other trees, capturing any light that managed to peek through the canopy above to the branches below. Most people who lived on Eleanor Place failed to realize how large it had grown as its trunk extended almost to the bottom of the ravine, where the creek's ample water supply sustained its longevity. The magnificent oak had grown to such a height that its treetop rose equal to the trees that had grown along the rim of the ravine where the houses were built. It blended into the growth of these newer trees in such a way that if you did not climb down the rocky hillside behind the houses, you would just assume that its base was near the top like most of the other trees.

Halfway up the tree was a large hole that had developed when a branch had been struck by lightning around the turn of the century, and the subsequent years of rain and cold had rotted away a large opening in the side of the mighty oak. The tree was prime real estate, from a raccoon family's point of view.

It was in this hollow that I was raised. I was the youngest in a litter of five. It was the last of six litters my mother would have in her lifetime.

Let's see, if I'm the fifth of five . . . times six litters . . . but mom had an average litter of four . . . well a little too much math for my liking, but it added up to the fact that I was nothing special. I was the last in a long line of raccoon children, many of whom were far too dumb to survive past the first couple of years of life.

Take my two sisters for example, they were not even six months old when they wandered into the Tyler family's back yard and into the waiting jaws of their Rottweiler. It gave me some sense of satisfaction and closure when the Aster's bought the place and tore it down.

The oldest of the litter was my brother Randy. He was crossing the road one night in an attempt to get an apple core someone had thrown out their car window. With a blinding flash of light, a Buick quickly reduced the number of children from our litter down to two.

My other brother was Derek. Of all the family members I would have chosen to have a date with a Buick it would have been him. He had a mean streak in him that, even though we lived together in the same household all our lives, still scared me a little. You know how when you are a kid and you are messing around with someone, maybe they put you in a headlock or give you a bite or something? Well, Derek would always cross the line from fun to scary, from being playful to inflicting pain. During most of my childhood, I had a bruise or a scratch or some other little memento somewhere on my body to remind me of my big brother. He was smart enough and tough enough not to be taken down by the things that got most raccoons.

In contrast, my survival depended more on a cautious mix of being afraid to try anything new and being lazy enough to not get myself into too many potentially dangerous situations. I was not exceptionally large, or fast, or smart by raccoon standards, just an average fellow. If I did have one skill, I would say that I was a good observer of the world around me and was able to pick up on the patterns of the happenings in the neighborhood. This proved to be most beneficial when it came time to get a snack. I knew exactly when the garbage trucks would come and the precise time the joggers would begin their day. I learned which trees produced which nut or seed and at what time and how often the coyotes or other predators would roam through the ravine looking for some unsuspecting animal to make a meal of. These skills enabled me to move through the area with a certain ease. It was rare that someone would spot me, human or otherwise, and if they did, it was usually while I was bidding a hasty retreat. I quickly became mom's favorite as my stealthy skills often meant I would bring something yummy home for the family to eat.

My father, on the other hand, was a hard one to impress. In my younger years, he was a good provider for the family and had a nose for sniffing out food from almost anywhere. He was never one to offer praise or to tell you that he was proud of you. You could tell him of the amazing thing you did that day, but he had a knack at pointing out the one thing you could have done that would have made it better. I remember one time when I was just a few months old I had come up with a foolproof plan to get into Mrs. Abrams' new garbage bin. It involved some chicken bones, a rope that I had scavenged, and a hub cap that we had found after it had rolled down the ravine and into the creek. I drew everything up with diagrams and detailed instructions to show my dad. I was convinced he would look at my plan, give a low whistle, and recognize the genius behind it. Then he would put his arms around me and tell how much he loved me. In reality, he barely glanced away from his newspaper to look at my plan. He gave a quick cursory turn of the head and then, in his dry tone — totally devoid of emotion — told me that it would never work. A few seconds later he was back to reading his paper and ignoring me.

I was devastated. The seeds of self-doubt and insecurity were now planted deep inside me, not that a child needs to be told that everything he does is wonderful and special. There is definitely a downside to a child venturing out into world thinking he can do no wrong, only to be met with the reality that he does in fact do wrong and repeatedly makes mistakes just like everyone else. I have spent considerable time though, wondering how different my life would have been, if he would have just stopped what he was doing, and given me just a few minutes of his undivided attention and validated any efforts I had made. *Maybe I would feel happy?* Even if flaws or problems had needed to be pointed out, at least I would have been open to being taught in those moments. But his emotional detachment inevitably caused me to implode into the darkness inside myself. Alas, it was not to be, and the brooding insecure Gary of my childhood came to be.

CHAPTER 10
Mitzy and Lulu

MITZY AND LULU WERE UTTERLY convinced that the universe revolved around them, safe in the lack of any evidence to the contrary. They ate their scratch-made meals from matching gold-rimmed bowls. Their beds were large, sumptuous pillows that, in terms of comfort, would be the envy of any creature, animal or human. Imported collars that cost as much as a man's suit graced their necks. Every conceivable dog toy money could buy was at their disposal.

Mitzy and Lulu spent most of the day basking in Mrs. Aster's attention. They quickly learned that she could easily be convinced to provide them with anything their hearts desired. She must have been a clever human because she only took a few months to learn most of her tricks; a bark and a circle — she would stop what she was doing and grab their sweaters and leashes to go on a walk; standing on the hind legs with sad eyes and a slow pawing of the air — she knew it was time to go and get a treat; sitting on the floor with a head cocked to the side and a soft whimper would always bring dinner right on time. Mrs. Aster was such a clever girl.

After the dogs got a little older Mrs. Aster insisted that the back yard be fenced in and an 'automatic canine egress device' be installed to allow Mitzy and Lulu to have access to the outdoors whenever they wanted; almost identical to a doggy door, only considerably more expensive. She was convinced that the dogs need a little fresh air from time to time. Convinced by whom was a question left for Mr. Aster to ponder.

There was another side to Mitzy and Lulu of which the Asters were unaware. Even the most pampered of dogs have a wild animal inside of them that needs expression from time to time. On some nights after the Asters fell into the deepest part of their sleep, Mitzy and Lulu would stealthily head out the doggy egress door and into the darkness of night. They had perfected leaving the bedroom without making the slightest of sounds. Upon entering the back yard, they had learned to stay close to the house so as not to trigger any of the motion-sensing floodlights. The goal was always the same, to make it to the far end of the yard to where the fence that separated the backyard and the ravine ran. In the corner, there were some large azalea bushes. Underneath the bushes was the fruit of months of their doggy labor: a Skye terrier sized tunnel that had been dug under the fence and out to the wilderness beyond.

CHAPTER 11

A Triumphant Return

WALKING OUT OF THE GARDEN, I had never felt so alive and exhilarated. The recent events kept playing over and over again in my mind in slow motion. The look of shock on Mr. Pickles face when the old lady took a swing at him would be etched into my memory forever. When I caught sight of Jenny waiting for me at the edge of the brambles, she seemed to be more excited than I was. Grinning from ear to ear, she hopped around and around in little circles, anticipating my return. When I was within arm's reach, she bowled me over and pinned me to the ground. "I told you it would work! I told you!" she crowed gleefully. "You were amazing! I almost died when Mr. Pickles caught you in the garden and I couldn't believe it when the old lady came to your defense!" She could hardly contain herself, and it felt good to make Jenny so happy. Upon seeing her unbridled enthusiasm for our recent success, I even found her 'I told you so' attitude to be quite endearing.

"Come on," I said, getting to my feet. "Let's not push our luck any more by staying out here where someone might see us." We headed into the opening at the base of the blackberry bushes, on to the path that would take us safely into the deeper parts of the forest. I could hear Jenny following from behind, and she had still not stopped talking. "Think of what this means! If you can impersonate Mr. Pickles, that means you can go wherever he goes! You can *become* him! Outside the house and *inside* the house!" The way she put the emphasis on the word inside caused the vision of Johnny twitching in his bed staring off at a spot on the wall to suddenly flash in my mind. I came to a stop and turned around to confront Jenny.

"Inside?" I said, my voice climbing an octave higher for no apparent reason. "Listen, Jenny, that was fun and everything, and I am just as surprised that it worked as anyone but *inside?* Don't you think that would be going too far?" I tried to regain the timbre in my voice in order to sound less like a coward and more like a man who was merely protesting out of common sense. "What would be the point?"

Jenny cut me off before I could get another word in. "What would be the point? Really? You have to ask that?" The look she gave me made me pause for a moment. *Was I missing something?* It dawned on her from the expression on my face that I did *not* understand the point, and that I hadn't thought much about the reason behind why we were doing all of this. My ignorance appeared to soften her indignation, and this was reflected in the tone of her next utterance. "What would be the point? Gary, do you realize what this ability of yours could mean for us? For everyone? Think of it . . ."

Jenny then proceeded to outline all the things we could do with this newfound ability to impersonate Mr. Pickles. No more eating out of trash cans or risking our lives to steal something from a garden. No more worrying about the terrible traps or potent poisons the humans used against us. No more hunger driving us deep into the woods to forage for food, only to face the danger of becoming someone else's dinner. It would mean fresh, high-quality meals whenever we wanted. It meant full access to all the fridges and pantries of Eleanor Place and maybe beyond. And it was not just about food; blankets and pillows and all the comforts humans had to offer could be ours. In time, we might even be able to access the warmth of a human's home on the coldest of winter nights. Jenny laid it all out with the art and skill of a master persuader. Each word and sentence were carefully organized to paint me a picture of all the good that I could accomplish for us, for our families and anyone else that might require our services. I could become the invisible bridge between two worlds, and the transporter of the humans' excesses to the forest creatures that needed them most.

The thought of Mrs. Abrams' warm hand stroking my fur came back to me. I had a vision of being curled up at her feet in front of a warm fire, my belly full of chicken and cream, the best of everything she had to offer. The wind would howl outside as a blizzard blanketed the area in several feet of snow. *Maybe I haven't thought of all the possibilities.*

The sound of Jenny's voice brought me back to the conversation at hand. "Listen, the possibilities are endless," she said, as if she had been reading my mind, "but it will not come without a lot of work. Come on, let's go back to my place and we'll figure out a plan of action."

As we walked back to Jenny's place I reflected on her words. It was true that we could do a lot of good together and help many of the other animals. But I could not help but notice that I would be the one required to take all the risks and to make all of the sacrifices. My disquieting thoughts got the best of me and I muttered aloud, "Why does it always come down to me to do the dirty jobs?" A pang of guilt for my self-pity hit me, so to cover my shame I quickly added, "I guess that is just my cross-eyed bear."

"Well, has to be someone," Jenny replied, "I guess you are the lucky one . . . wait . . . what did you just say?"

"That I do the dirty . . ."

"No not that. You used an expression . . ." Jenny looked at me, waiting for me to fill in the words.

"I said that's my cross-eyed bear."

"That's the one! That's what I thought you said. You know that's not how it goes." Jenny folded her arms and looked at me with an expression of incredulity.

"Sure it is. It makes perfect sense. What did you think it was?" I asked her.

"The saying is: 'that's the cross I bear'. It means to carry the burden of suffering for others . . ." Jenny's voice trailed off a little.

"Well I agree. That is the meaning I was referring to. But yours doesn't make any sense. How does making a bear cross at you have anything to do with suffering or helping others?" I asked her sincerely.

"No, not cross like angry; cross like two pieces of wood laid at opposing angles. You know — a cross." The agitation in her voice started to increase.

"How on earth would you lay down two giant bears at opposing angles? They would eat you! Let alone being able to get them to lie still enough to pull it off. That doesn't make a lick of sense! No, no, it's definitely, 'cross-eyed bear'. Can you imagine how hard it would be to go through life as a cross-eyed bear?" Gary did his best impression of what he thought it might look like, trying hard to stare at the tip of his nose, all the while seeing if he could get his eyes to cross. "You're supposed to be a feared apex predator! Even the animals you ate would be cracking up as they died! Plus, with that long snout they have, they would be staring at the end of their noses for their entire life. Like a camera with a permanent thumb in the frame. That's the kind of suffering I'm talking about!"

Jenny stared in silent disbelief, unable to reply to the dizzying yet some-how flawless display of logic she had just witnessed. With that, the conversation was over, and we headed back to Jenny's place in silence, each of us lost in our thoughts of the day's events and what the future had in store.

CHAPTER 12
The Jackson Family

ETHAN AND FELICITY JACKSON'S STORY was something you might read in a children's story book about young love. Everyone who saw them said that they looked so good together — a perfect match. He was the hunky football star, six-feet tall, square-jawed with dark brown hair, and she was the perky cheerleader with blonde hair and pale blue eyes, of course. Isn't that the message of those stories? If the prince is dashing, and the girl is beautiful — albeit in distress — it is an inevitable conclusion that they will share a kiss and live happily ever after. Even in the stories about animals, the hideous avian did not find happiness until he became an attractive adult.

They had liked each other in middle school, and they dated in high school. Felicity, convinced that she had found true love, dreamed of the wedding, the children, and the little house with the white picket fence. She had the next ten years of their life all planned out, and it appeared to their friends and families that they were living a fairy tale.

The dream was shattered when Ethan went off to college. His plan was a career in the big city, with all the excitement that comes from living in a place where everything doesn't close before it even gets dark outside. His plan was that as soon as he graduated and got his high paying job, he would get an amazing apartment somewhere downtown. Felicity would then move in with him and they would eventually get married.

They would finally escape the small town where they had grown up and thrive in the excitement and bright lights of the big city.

They had promised each other that they would keep in touch daily and visit each other on weekends and all of the holidays. Unfortunately for them both, despite the promises and plans, reality quickly set in and they had broken up during his freshman year. It looked like there would be no happy ending to their fairy tale romance after all.

As tragic as the end of their romance was, it was equally surprising when the relationship started up again. After Ethan graduated from college, the high paying job and amazing apartment in the city never materialized. Despite countless interviews and an unpaid internship, he was living in a dank basement with mountains of debt. Eventually, the money ran so low he had to work at a coffee shop just to have enough to eat.

A man who cannot see his future will often look to his past. This was true of Ethan. The small town that he could not wait to leave just a few years prior, was now calling him home and felt safe and inviting. He returned to live with his parents while he took some time to rethink his future. The girl that he had left behind never looked better, and his romance with Felicity was rekindled. The two eventually married, and Ethan found work nearby. Felicity's dream was revived — albeit with an asterisk — and she poured her heart into becoming the perfect family.

Just like the dream of the storybook romance, the dream of the perfect family proved to be much more difficult to obtain than Felicity imagined. After their son Thomas was born, she was soon overwhelmed with the responsibility of being a new mother. Some say that being a parent is the hardest job there is. It is not that each aspect of being a parent is difficult. Feed the baby — check. Change the baby — check. Put the baby down for a nap — check. Each job in itself was easy and enjoyable enough, but what makes parenting so difficult is the unrelenting nature of the tasks.

It is like being a marathon runner, only you can't stop running and the race has no finish line. *Dear God, please let him go down for a nap. I just need thirty minutes of rest to keep my sanity!* Of course, those were the days the baby would never sleep, and the cries would continue without ceasing.

This, of course, put a strain on the marriage of Ethan and Felicity. He would arrive home exhausted from work, expecting to be rewarded for his efforts with a good hot meal and a little attention from his wife. Instead, he was greeted with a wife on the edge and left-overs he had to warm up himself. She, expecting that the cavalry had finally arrived, would be pushed over the precipice by his self-centered behavior and lack of interest in caring for their beautiful child.

The evening would often proceed with him complaining and her begging for some help. At some point, for the sake of her self-preservation, she would thrust into his arms the screaming child who was in obvious need of a changing. *What does she do all day? I am the one slaving away so that she can have it easy staying home.* These were the thoughts passing through his head as he awkwardly attempted to change the diaper, his face recoiling in disgust from the smell. The reason they are still married today is that he never uttered those thoughts out loud, maybe out of wisdom, probably out of fear.

In reality, they were both out of touch with the sacrifices the other was making for the benefit of the family. They were at a breaking point — both physically and emotionally — when Felicity's mother arrived for a visit. She was the option play that they both desperately needed, and it finally gave Felicity a chance to stop running and get some rest. Ethan was never a fan of his mother-in-law — she always had too many opinions for his liking — but now he appreciated her more than any other person he could think of.

Felicity eventually got a handle on the duties that came with motherhood. She found comfort and success in a positive attitude and a strict schedule when it came to caring for young Thomas. By the time their daughter Emily came along, she was running a tight ship and broadcasting online the secrets of her domestic success. Her pictures were gorgeous, perfectly framed, and always with a bright splash of color. Thomas and Emily were posed and re-posed, over and over until they were captured in the perfect shot. Her followers quickly grew, and she basked in her newfound notoriety and the financial rewards that came with it. Soon her day was less about taking care of the children and more about showing other mothers what the perfect home and family looked like.

It was at this point in their lives that the 'incident' happened. It was a warm spring day and Felicity was thinking about doing a photo shoot outside with the children. "The sun is perfect this time of day near the tulip beds," she told the children as she combed their hair and straightened up their outfits. "Now you kids go outside and wait for me by the garden. Mommy just has to go and get her camera." With that she shoved the children out the door and into the back yard under threat of severe punishment should they dirty their clothes or mess up their hair. As she ran to get her photography equipment, she could not resist checking her online accounts again to see how many likes she had already received today, and if anyone had left any positive reviews.

Thomas and Emily headed towards the flowers, patiently awaiting their mother's return. As they approached the tulips, they both noticed something moving in the garden. It turned out that one of the local skunks was foraging in the soil for grubs and worms. The children were delighted to see the skunk; their mother would not let them have a pet, as it would make too much of a mess in the house. The skunk for his part was indifferent to the children; they seemed to be of no threat, and there were far too many delicious and distracting things to eat. The three of them were happy to coexist, that is until Felicity Jackson entered the scene.

The minute that Felicity saw the skunk she let out a blood-curdling scream. Judging by the intensity of her response, any normal person would have thought that the children were being murdered. Alas, it was only a skunk, and a distracted skunk at that. "Thomas, Emily, get into the house NOW!" she screamed. Their mother's reaction caught them both off guard, as neither of them had sensed the immediate danger that their mother had. "GET INSIDE!" she kept screaming. Thomas and Emily slowly backed away from the tulip garden. They both casually turned and headed back inside the house.

Once the children were safe inside, Felicity decided to wage war against the skunk. She threw anything she could find in the skunk's direction. Even the lawn chairs became weapons in the hands of Felicity Jackson. The skunk himself was quite confused at this point. Here it was a lovely day for having a little snack in among the tulips, then the next thing you know a hysterical woman is hurling everything in sight in your general direction.

The skunk bid a hasty retreat out of the garden and out of the Jacksons' back yard. The conclusion for Felicity Jackson was not as simple. She fell to the grass on her knees after the skunk had left, sobbing into her hands, still shaking from the trauma she had just experienced. After a long day's work, it was to this scene that Ethan Jackson arrived. "What happened?" he asked as he ran out to his trembling wife. "There was a terrible, dirty creature and it almost attacked the children!" she blurted out between the tears. "Oh Ethan, what are we going to do? We just can't have these wild animals running around near our children!" Ethan was a smart enough man to know that now was not the time to argue with his wife. "Don't worry Felicity. I will find a way to get rid of all of those awful, awful creatures," he said as he held her reassuringly. Again and again he repeated, "don't worry, we'll get rid of them all." He might have consoled his wife a little more quietly had he realized that two impressionable little minds were intently listening from behind the planter nearby.

CHAPTER 13

A Break in the Case

MAX AND JONATHAN HAD FINISHED interviewing everyone they could without developing a single lead. They did not find any information that shed light on the location of the Possum family, or who might have been responsible for their disappearance. Max's abundantly clever fox brain was churning through all the available facts when a break came their way. Jonathan's sister Amber came scampering through the woods and headed straight for them. She was a chipmunk who might be equal to Jonathan's intelligence, even if she had not yet mastered the arts of patience and discretion like he had.

"Jonathan! Jonathan! Come quickly! Something shocking has been found down by the creek! I think you better come take a look!" No sooner had she delivered the message, she turned around to head back in the opposite direction, pausing only to urge them to follow and to try to keep up. Max and Jonathan followed her through the trees and down into the depths of the ravine, on one of the trails the larger animals had carved out in the forest. They walked for what seemed to be hours, along the trail, and down to the deeper, less accessible areas of the ravine, far beyond the view of any of the homes on Eleanor Place. The closer they got to the creek the thicker and more impassable the dense undergrowth became. Moisture-loving broadleaf plants that could take advantage of the tiniest amounts of sunlight had taken over the area. The smell of decomposing plants and rich, fertile soil filled the air. The ground was damp, as it was not the kind of place that would ever really dry out. Max's soft, copper-colored fur was getting wetter and wetter as he passed between the ferns and the damp undergrowth. He was beginning to regret his decision to follow Amber without first getting more details about their destination. "How much further?" he heard Jonathan call to his sister. *Poor fellow*, Max thought to himself. *The long journey must have been even more difficult for him, being so small.*

"Just a few more minutes," came the reply from Amber. "It's just around the next bend." The flow of the river picked up speed the further downstream they descended. Recent rains had swollen the small tributaries upstream. The creek had now narrowed causing the stream's flow to quicken to the point that Max, upon seeing the raging waters, had decided he would not dare to try and wade across. As they rounded the corner, a slight drop in the creek bed made for a small waterfall. Over the years, the waterfall had hollowed out a little pool. A small sand bar had formed where the pool outflowed and formed a bend. From that point on, the creek bed widened, and the flow of the water became gentler.

"Just beyond the pool on the sandbar. Can you see it? That's where we're heading," Amber's voice called out, trying to penetrate the sound of the rushing water. The trio made their way past the pool and found a spot where they could safely climb down and get on to the sandbar. "Maggie Mink was the one who made the discovery," Amber began to explain. We could see two dark, wet lumps on the sandbar as we made our way closer. "She was patrolling up and down the river looking for snacks when she came across the bodies." As the words left Amber's mouth, we could make out that the forms on the sandbar were the bodies of two adult possums. Max and Jonathan approached the crime scene carefully, trying not to disturb the area and any evidence it might contain. Judging by the way the bodies were swollen and bloated it was clear that they had been in the river for more than a few days. The recent rains must have washed them downstream for a while before they came to rest on this particular spot of the sandbar.

"They appear to be the possums we've been looking for," Jonathan surmised. "Of course, we will need to do a closer examination to be sure."

"Notice the white markings on the female," Max said, pointing to the smaller of the two bodies. "I noticed them in the photographs back at the house. She has unique markings for a possum, more grey around the eyes and on the forehead, I am quite sure it is them. Now the big question is: Who or what killed them? All that time floating in the river is not going to make our job any easier." Max was cautiously examining the area as he approached the body of the male possum.

The body lay on its side, curled up as one might imagine a possum to be if he were taking a nap in a sunbeam on a lazy afternoon. Starting at the tail, Max looked for any indication as to the cause of their demise, a puncture wound, or some other indication of parasites or disease. When he reached the head, he still had no clear indication of what might have happened. *Some kind of poison maybe?*

It was then that he noticed an indentation on the side of the male possum's head that had sunk into the soft sand of the river. "Jonathan, grab some sticks and help me roll this body over!" As Max waited, a sinking feeling was starting to develop in his gut. Jonathan scampered over to his vulpine friend, carrying a couple of sticks which they placed under the possum and then joined forces to lift and roll the body over on to its other side. Immediately the cause of death became visible. "Looks like someone came up behind him on the left side and struck him on the head with something. The way the skull is caved in, it looks like it was a particularly violent blow, maybe a rock or some other object?"

"Do you think floating down the creek could have caused that kind of damage? Maybe his skull was damaged after he was already dead," Jonathan pondered out loud. He was searching for a more palatable reason than murder.

"No, these other scratches and wounds to the hands and feet were most likely from the creek, but this damage to the skull was far too violent to be caused by the river. I would guess that even another possum would have trouble causing damage like this. It was most likely something much bigger and stronger than him." Max was mentally running through a list of creatures that might be powerful enough to do this kind of damage. Humans, of course, were always at the top of the list. "I think we can rule out a predator like a coyote or a bear. There is no other damage to the body. No one has made a meal out of this guy; just killed him and then pushed him into the creek or left him close enough to the edge of the creek that the rain did the pushing. Let's take another look at the female."

Max and Jonathan carefully examined the body of the other possum. It too had damage to the skull by a blunt object, which was most likely the cause of death. The damage was more to the frontal lobe and it was much more severe. Max surmised the husband was killed first — most likely in a surprise attack from behind — and then the attacker came at the wife, who by then would have turned to defend herself, only to be overpowered and subsequently struck with multiple blows to the front of her skull. A gruesome business indeed, all of this was.

"What do you think happened to the children?" Jonathan asked. "I don't see any evidence of their bodies at all." While Max was examining the crime scene Jonathan had taken the opportunity to have a good look in both directions up and down the stream. "Do you think there's any chance some of them survived?" A flicker of hope crept into Jonathan's voice for the first time that afternoon.

"Not likely," Max quickly extinguished the idea. "If the children had survived, they would have gone back to the home or to a nearby friend or family member to seek help and shelter. Someone would have seen or heard something. Our canvassing of the area around the possums' home ruled out that possibility. It's more likely the killer moved on to the easier targets of the children after he dispatched the parents. The bodies would have been much smaller and lighter and would not have got caught up on this shallow area here," he gestured to the parents' current resting place. "The children easily could have been swept so far downstream that we will never find them. Unless of course . . ." his voice trailed off.

"Unless of course what?" Jonathan was not sure he even wanted to hear the answer.

"Unless of course, the killer had something else in mind for them," Max decided to leave it at that. "Come on, we don't have much afternoon light left to work with. I don't think there's anything more we can learn here today. We will give the bodies a proper burial and head home before it gets too dark." With that Max, Jonathan and Amber began their solemn task. None of them spoke another word until they were back on the trail and heading home.

CHAPTER 14
The Making of a Hero

AFTER WALKING IN SILENCE THROUGH the forest behind Mrs. Abrams' property, we eventually arrived at a spacious bunny burrow tucked into the side of a hill. The entrance was well concealed by two large rocks leaning against each other, allowing for a perfect rabbit-sized opening. Jenny had been raised there, the youngest in what would be considered a large family, even by rabbit standards. After her parents died suddenly, one by one her siblings spread out looking for greener pastures, leaving the family home to Jenny. She had lived there all alone in that big burrow ever since.

It was a nice home, in a good location of the forest, where many of the other animals had decided to reside. The area offered many amenities, including a dense thicket of trees and bushes, as well a food and water nearby. The difficult terrain made it harder for the larger animals to navigate through, and so the area became a sought-after location by the smaller creatures of the forest as it was a safe place to find shelter.

If you ventured further into the forest the landscape changed to become a large, grassy meadow. A creek ran through the middle and provided both food and water to everyone who lived nearby. A large boulder with the comparable dimensions of a minivan sat conspicuously in the center of the meadow near the creek. The animals had named it elephant rock due to its relative size and shape compared to a resting pachyderm, as if the great creature had decided to lay down in the grass, never to move again.

A couple of squirrel families had built nests high up in the trees around Jenny's place. Porcupines and possums had also settled nearby, and a family of badgers lived in a burrow that had been excavated decades ago. Multiple generations of the badger family had lived there over the years, and at present, a large group of descendants of the original builders still occupied the impressive heritage home. It was quite famous among all the badgers in the area (at least that is what I had been told). I had played there as a young child as my mother had been friends with the matriarch of the badger family. At the time she had two children of her own, and our parents thought it would be beneficial if we socialized together. I had spent many an afternoon getting into trouble with those two. They would be grown now, and no doubt had families of their own that still occupied the home. The badger burrow consisted of an unusually large, open chamber, filled with natural light from a series of small tunnels that let in the light but not the rain. Numerous side chambers served as sleeping quarters, and food storage areas had been dug out over the generations. Rumor had it that there were even secret tunnels that had been dug ages ago and that were now long forgotten, concealed by the ever-shifting earth and the resulting collapses of some of the passageways. One could only imagine what treasures were hidden down there.

We entered Jenny's place and closed the door behind us. When I looked around it was obvious that she had turned the main living area into some kind of situation room. There were multiple whiteboards attached to the walls in her living room with all kinds of writings and diagrams in various colors. A large bulletin board was set up with sketches she had made of Mr. Pickles, the Asters' Skye terriers, and a host of the other animals and humans that lived in the neighborhood. Another board had a rough map of Eleanor Place and its various homes, with features such as cat doors, broken fences, and other useful information she had gathered about the dwellings. Multiple red and green arrows, sometimes pointing in at the homes and yards, sometimes pointing out, had been scrawled all over the map.

Of all the drawings that she had posted on the boards, what disturbed me most were life-sized images of myself, depicted from all four sides. Walking over to get a better view, my eyes fixated on one of the profile views. *Do I always look like that?* I reached out with my hand to trace the outline of my back. Undeniably it arched a little in what some may call . . . a hump. Below the illustrations, there was a small table where a variety of masks, hats and other garments had been laid out. A basket on the table held hair dyes, combs, and other accessories.

"Jenny . . . what is all of this?" I asked in stunned disbelief. "Why do you have a life-sized image of me and my backside in your living room?" I couldn't help but be grateful that my tail was down in the rear-view picture. That is one asterisk that nobody needed a reference to.

Jenny hopped over and rubbed up against me. "Well, one day I got the idea that you would look a lot like Mr. Pickles if you did not have your black mask markings, and I wondered if you could impersonate him. Once I decided that it was possible for you to become the cat . . ." she softened her voice before delivering the rest of her plan, "I got to wondering how many other animals you could impersonate. Then this . . ." she gestured broadly to the entire room for dramatic effect, ". . . all kind of happened. What do you think?" She let her long, soft ears droop down alongside her face and looked at me with her wide, hopeful eyes. I felt like I should be angry at her, but looking at Jenny, I just could not bring any of those emotions to the fore.

I needed to stall for time, as my thoughts and feelings were whirling about within me and I was unsure how to respond. My feelings for Jenny were clashing with my lack of self-esteem and my fear of the unknown. In one thought I was flattered by the attention I was receiving, and in the next, it felt like I was in some kind of crazy dream. I started fumbling with one of the masks on the nightstand and feeling the soft, smooth fabric between my fingers. I kept my gaze fixed firmly upon the mask, so as to avoid eye contact with Jenny.

"You're not mad at me, are you?" Hearing the sadness in her voice, my first instinct was to try and reassure her. *No. Wait. This is all insane. How can I just ignore all of this? I thought today was just a spur of the moment thing and now I find out she has been planning this all along? Who does she think she is? Who does she think I am?*

I just kept looking at the mask, turning it over and over, not knowing what to say. Jenny came over and stood silently beside me, reached her paws out to take hold of my hands, and stilled my nervous fumbling of the mask. "Look at me," her voice was kind but firm. "If you are upset or angry, this can all go away today. We can pack everything up, and I will never mention it again." Her soothing words helped me to gain a bit of control over my emotions. When she looked at me, she gave me a subtle smile. "Gary, I want you to know that all of this was not just some crazy idea or wild scheme." She paused to pivot the conversation from an impassioned defense to an expression of genuine conviction. "All of this is because I believe in you, and I believe that you have great potential; the potential to help people and to change the lives of those who live around you. If only you had the means . . . I know you would use it to help those who need it the most."

Despite her inspiring words of confidence in me, my thoughts drifted back to our success in Mrs. Abrams' garden. A pang of guilt came over me as I remembered that when I first realized what we had accomplished, my only thought was of how I could keep myself warm and fill my own belly with food. In the shadow of my self-indulgence, I did not feel qualified for the role of the altruistic hero, and I certainly did not see myself the way Jenny had just described me. "Jenny, I do not think I am the man you think I am." As I spoke, I could no longer endure her gaze, so I cast my eyes upon the floor. "I think you are making me out to be something that I am not." My head and shoulders slumped a little as I started to turn away from Jenny.

"Maybe you don't see it in yourself," she said as she put her paw softly on my shoulder, "but I see it in you. I see the kindness in your eyes and how you put others ahead of yourself. You may not see it Gary, but I can see the man that you can become. I think you can do extraordinary things! And I want to help you, if you will let me."

In one brief moment, Jenny had expressed something I had longed to hear my entire life, as if someone had finally cleaned and bandaged a gaping, open wound. There is something inspiring about hearing that someone believes in you, and it ignited a small flicker of hope inside me — a flicker that I only now realized had been extinguished long ago.

As a child, I had an inborn desire to do something good — as I believe most children have — and to be a hero to those around me. In my play, I would take on the role of healer, bandaging the imaginary wounds of those I loved. Or I would become a rescuer, saving my family from a burning inferno; or a gatherer and a preparer of food that would feed and nourish those closest to me. And on occasion, I would picture myself with some kind of superpower — incredible strength or the ability to fly — that made me a hero with the ability to protect and change the lives of those around me when they were powerless to do it for themselves. Quite often an innate desire to do something good and help others finds expression through the play of children.

In the end, instead of doing all the wonderful, unselfish deeds I had imagined as a child, the desire to help others that once burned within had gradually been extinguished without me even realizing it. It slowly crept into my identity that I did not hold much worth, only to be reinforced from time to time by disparaging remarks from those whose support I needed the most. It was further bolstered by a world that praises mundane accomplishments and values the accumulation of possessions over any of the qualities that would truly make one a hero. My life had become centered on satisfying my personal needs and wants to the point that I was taking a little more than I gave, and I was living a life without a clear purpose. The hero inside of me had slowly faded away like a cooling ember and had been replaced by an imperceptible sadness.

Hearing Jenny say that she believed in me, that she saw something good inside of me, was as if someone blew on that dying ember and stoked the fire of possibility again. While I realize that I might not be anything special or have anything about me that makes me better than anyone else, it does not mean that as an average person I cannot do anything good. You do not need any superpowers to think about the world around you, to notice the needs of others and to reach out and help; to simply *be* good. And if the potential to be a true hero resides in all of us, in the choices we make every day, then that means none of us are so special that we deserve to take from others the very things we desire for ourselves. We bear an undeniable responsibility to one another.

I turned back to face her and said "I am not sure what you see in me Jenny. I am not sure I even see those things myself." I paused for a moment, to the point that the silence became a little uncomfortable. Mustering up the courage, I looked into Jenny's eyes and said, "If you think I can do it . . . I am willing to try." With those words, Jenny threw her arms around me and our adventure was about to begin.

CHAPTER 15

Mr. and Mrs. Williams

MR. AND MRS. WILLIAMS HAD lived next door to Mrs. Abrams for close to forty years. They had bought the small bungalow shortly after they had married, and quickly got to the work of turning it into a home. Otis Williams was a hardworking man with skills in carpentry and mechanics. Esther Williams was a kind woman with an old soul who loved to spend the afternoon listening to whatever people were willing to share with her over a nice cup of tea.

They raised three children in their home on Eleanor Place. Their firstborn was a son named Michael, in honor of Esther's father. Two years later their daughter Eliza was born. The birth was not an easy one, and Otis Williams was grateful not to be raising two small children on his own. The youngest child Adelaide was a bit of a late surprise, being born seven years after Eliza.

Otis took great pride in taking care of their home. The house was heritage yellow with white trim around the doors and windows. He took the time to paint it every few years, just to keep it looking sharp. The gardens out front had been expanded over time and gave the house the feeling of an old English cottage. Otis had made various trellises and garden arches for his wife, and they dotted the property and pathways around the property. Everything was a bit overgrown now, from the roses to the trees and the climbing vines, but in her younger years, Esther's gardens were almost as famous as her award-winning pies. Around the back of the home, the yard was quite large and continued to widen as you got closer to the Abrams farm, staying relatively flat until the hill rose at the back of the property. The open area had been fenced many years ago, and at an earlier time Otis Jackson kept some livestock in the field, including sheep and cows.

As they got older and the area got built up, the livestock went except for a dozen or so chickens that Mr. Williams still kept for the fresh eggs. "I am not going to eat those store-bought eggs!" he would always say in a gruff way, "they just don't taste right!" The chickens kept to themselves most of the time and lived in a little shed that Otis had built as a present to Esther on their seventh wedding anniversary. Needless to say, it was not the most romantic gift he ever gave her, and he spent the next thirty-some years being reminded of his mistake.

"Did I ever tell you what Otis got me for our seventh anniversary?" Esther loved to bring the subject up whenever the topic of romance or marriage or anniversaries came along. "He gave me a chicken coop! I had been dropping hints for weeks about a pair of earrings I saw down at the department store in the city. I even took Otis over to see them one time and told him how much I liked them, but he didn't get the hint. When he put a blindfold on me and said he wanted me to go outside to show me my anniversary gift, I thought to myself, *oh my God, he went and got me a car instead of those earrings!* To my shock and dismay do you know what I opened my eyes to? A chicken coop! That's right, a chicken coop! Isn't that the worst gift you could imagine? For my anniversary, I got both the chore of cleaning up the poop of some birds and the means to have to make Otis breakfast every day of my life!" Fortunately, the marriage and the chicken coop were both built soundly enough to survive down to this day.

The chickens did not roam too often, most of the time they were content to stay near the coop and scratch around at the base of the trees in the back of the yard. Occasionally they would come up into the gardens around the house, but the family's chocolate lab Teddy loved to give chase and send them running back to the safety of the chicken coop. Teddy was no longer with them but the lessons he dealt out stuck in the minds of the chickens and had even been passed down from generation to generation. The only time the chickens would venture near the house would be if Otis forgot to give them food or fresh water.

Most of the neighbors did not mind the birds, even as the area transitioned from a rural setting to more of a suburb. Everyone realized that the Williams had been there forever, and out of respect for their history in the area, did not make much of a fuss about a few chickens, that is everyone except Felicity Jackson.

CHAPTER 16

Estranged

FEELING THE WARMTH OF JENNY'S arms and hearing her say that she believed in who I am had an inspiring effect on me. In my childhood, I had craved the kind of reassurance and security I was feeling at that moment.

After my brother and my sisters had died, my father spiraled down into a deep despair and on to a path of self-destruction. For a while, he had tried to pretend that everything was fine and that nothing bothered him. But watching as his life crumbled down around us, we had ample evidence to the contrary. Unable to deal with the loss of three more of his children, he turned to food and alcohol to deaden his pain. For a time, he would still try to go foraging at night to bring something home to feed his family. But more and more, his time and energy were being spent pursuing the things that temporarily soothed his pain. Often mom would catch him hoarding some of the unhealthier foods he would scavenge instead of sharing it with the family. He would find an old bag of marshmallows picked from a trash can, or a stale half-eaten banana cream pie plucked from Mrs. Aster's compost pile and then conceal them before he even entered the front door. When he thought we were asleep and no one was watching, he would head out at night and gorge himself on the things he had stashed away.

His unhealthy habits progressively took more and more control over his life, and it became apparent that he was either unwilling, or incapable of changing them. Mom tried to help by confronting him and interrogating him whenever he was out of her sight for too long. "What is that stain on your fur? Have you been eating something?" This often was the beginning of what would turn into a heated argument. He would at first try to be aloof and evasive. Mom would just press harder for the answers. He would then turn to a strategy of lying and denying. Mom would counter with confronting and accusing. Then dad would do what any raccoon does when he is backed into a corner. He would snarl and hiss and the whole thing would explode into a full-on fight. Mom's motives were in the right place, but in hindsight, and with eyes of an adult, I can see that her methods only drove the wedge between them even deeper. Of course, there are times when we need to respectfully point things out to our partners, especially if they are unaware of those things themselves, or cannot see the effects that their choices are having on the people around them. However, a constant drone of complaining does very little to change or improve anything and usually cements in stone the very cycle the complaints are trying to break.

What is often forgotten when we magnify the failings of the ones we love is that we already have our own inner voices providing us with all the criticism we could ever need. To break free, what we need most is someone who believes in us and who can be the light at the end of the tunnel. A good partner is someone who cheers our successes and inspires us to do more, not one that harps on our failings and is constantly reminding us of how we do not measure up. For my father, eating was a symptom of a much deeper issue. Being constantly confronted and badgered about it just drove the behavior into the shadows; his goal was not to change his destructive actions but to avoid being caught. He just kept spiraling down to a deeper and darker place.

Things continued to get worse for us as food alone was soon not enough to bury his feelings. He started patrolling the street on recycling day looking for any liquor bottles that found their way into the bins. They were empty of course from a human point of view, but the taste or two that remained at the bottom of the bottle was more than enough for a raccoon to get hammered on. With summertime and barbecues in full swing, dad's drinking got even more out of control. Half-full bottles of beer and cups of wine forgotten in people's back yards would easily fuel the addiction of a daring raccoon with nothing to lose and a taste for the sauce.

The father that would stumble home on those nights — mouth stained purple by the Aster's expensive cabernet sauvignon or reeking from the smell of too much beer — became increasingly aggressive and occasionally violent towards his family. He would chitter and snarl at mom the minute he saw her — a pre-emptive strike I imagine. At first, she would screech back, but his bared teeth and the back of his paw across her face a few times left her frightened and afraid of the man she once loved.

Day by day my brother's resentment of my father grew. I am not sure if he was brave or stupid, but unlike my approach, which was to lay low and stay unnoticed, he would often choose a direct confrontation with our father. This put my older brother in the crosshairs of my father's rage, and more often than not, on the receiving end of his outbursts. Maybe he was driven by a desire to protect my mother and thought that by attracting our father's anger toward himself he would spare her. Or maybe it was just his hatred of the man, and what he had become, that fueled the unending battles. Most of the conflicts ended with my brother seething with anger, then scampering off to lick his wounds.

As my brother grew larger and stronger, the rage inside of him grew as well. He became moody and withdrawn. Not that it was all bad, sometimes we would play a game or just talk, about the family, about life and the future. In those rare moments he would let his guard down and I could see that he was a raccoon who was vulnerable and hurting.

The last time I saw my brother was their final showdown. Dad had stumbled home and started screeching at mom. My brother — who by this point had grown to be almost as big as dad — decided enough was enough. Instead of the usual hissing and snarling, this time he lunged straight at dad and bit him on the forearm. "GET OUT!" he screamed, "YOU LOUSY DRUNK! NO ONE WANTS YOU AROUND HERE ANYMORE!" It was as if a mighty volcano of rage had exploded in the middle of our living room. The sudden attack caught my father by surprise, and he stumbled backward and screamed in pain. My brother turned for another strike but there is nothing like adrenaline and pain to sober one up quickly. My father was ready this time and braced for his attack, catapulting him to the floor near the entrance of our home with a mighty blow to his neck. My brother, stunned and shaken by the force of the retaliation, made the critical mistake of pausing to gather himself. No matter how strong and invincible you feel when you are a teenager, there is no substitute for the strength and experience of a grown man. My father was on top of him in a flash and held him there on the floor. No matter how much my brother screamed and howled, he was pinned and unable to get free. He cursed and he swore, and he spewed out all the hate and bile that he had pent up inside of himself and hurled it in the direction of my father, who was still sitting on his back. In the end, it was futile. Despite his efforts to escape he was still splayed out and humiliated, red-faced with anger and screaming with rage. I distinctly remember the chilling fear I felt wondering if I would ever have to bear the brunt of that madness.

My father continued to pin my brother down and held him there until his rants decreased in volume and intensity and his struggling eased. Neither one of them quite knew what to do next, so my father eventually made the first move. He shoved Derek's face hard into the floor in what was his most effective communication in a long time. He then backed off from my brother and braced for any counterattack. He did not need to worry, as Derek was in no position to strike. Disgraced and defeated, he stood up and brushed himself off. With no strength left in him to continue the battle, no path forward for peace, his only option was to leave. So he turned and headed out the door, not even gathering any of his belongings. He paused slightly, just enough time to take one last look back at my father and then at me and mom. Without saying a word, he just slipped out the door and into the night. That was the last time I ever saw him.

I often thought about the events of that night, and concluded that my brother must have pictured a sequence of events that would have ended with him standing over the defeated body of my father as the hero and savior of the family. With our father dethroned, he would have been the one to slink off in shame, knowing that he could never return to harm anyone again with my brother as the family's protector.

At least that is how I imagined it. It is all too easy to romanticize one's own past. The roles of hero and villain are neatly ascribed, as are the motives of the players involved. Complex interactions are reduced to mere good or evil. The possible outcomes of a different choice become idealized in our minds and the imagined results seem bereft of any negative consequences. The same kind of thinking often comes into play during bouts of loneliness or while having trouble in one's romantic life. In retrospect, the relationships not pursued seem to shine brighter and missed connections are fantasized into some something more meaningful, leaving one weighed down with the emotional burden of 'what could have been, what should have been, but was not'.

The reality is that one's past was never that simple. Relationships are only abandoned after weighing all the information available at that moment in time. All of the possible outcomes considered become an ever-branching pathway of different choices ultimately arriving at a decision — one that is impossible to know the final outcome of — which is as much the product of instinct and emotion as it is of reasoning and thinking ability. Even the choice of inaction produces consequences that will often build — like try-ing to hold back the water in a river — until the force becomes so great, it sweeps us along to a conclusion whether we wanted to go there or not. Since the task of knowing all of the potential outcomes is next to impos-sible, it becomes clear that it is not the choice that is ultimately the most important thing, but it is our commitment and attitude after the decision has been made that will determine if we are happy and satisfied or not.

The missed romance that we are now looking back at and dreaming of a different outcome for, might have been successful if in the past we were willing to take the chances needed to move it forward or to make the personal sacrifices that would have made a difference. The reality is — for whatever reason — when we had the opportunity to influence a different outcome, we made the choice not to. Now, in the sepia-toned light of the past, all of those nuances fall away, and a simpler, unrealisti-cally successful outcome is imagined.

Maybe that was the lens through which I was remembering my brother. I had always dismissed his violent outburst and anger and cast him in the role of hero. The fact was, both he and my father bore responsibility for the events that led to their final confrontation. For my brother it was in his daily decisions to respond to my father with resentment and rage. For my father it was in his habitual selfishness and his choice to lash out at his family rather than finding another way to deal with his pain.

While my brother's actions did not result in the victory he wanted, they did mark a turning point in our family. My father turned his anger inward after my brother left. He became increasingly aloof and distant, spending more and more of his time outside of our home. In the end, through his bad decisions, he unwittingly brought about the conclusion my brother had longed for. In one of his drunken nights, he wandered in through the side door of a garage that had not been fully closed in search of some more libations. As he was scavenging for more of the alcohol he craved, he stumbled upon a new drink — a delicious yellow/green liquid in a container labeled 'ethylene glycol' — and proceeded to drink its contents. Sometimes having hands that can open anything is not an advantage. That night our home had finally found some peace, but even the dead leave their mark upon the living. My mother, overwhelmed with anger and grief, was never the same.

CHAPTER 17

The Big Test

JENNY AND I SPENT HOURS, which soon became days, planning and scheming how to make my alternate personas into a believable reality. Her place was strewn with dyes and fabric and anything else we could think of that would help us to create the disguises I could use to impersonate the creatures that lived in the homes and forest around us.

At the end of the third day, Jenny and I had perfected five impersonations. We got porcupine easily as the movements and size were remarkably similar to a raccoon. Jenny would still have to make a quill jacket that I could slip into, but the key to making it work was a fake nose she created that would slip over mine. It would turn the pointiness of my face into the more porcine features needed to make it look authentic. The nose also came with the added bonus of hiding my whiskers, a much-preferred alternative to Jenny's first suggestion — shaving them off.

A skunk was another impression that only needed minor modifications due to our similar size and shape. I would indeed be a large skunk, but it looked convincing enough. Jenny said the larger size would only serve our purposes, as anyone I met would give me a wide berth, reducing the chances of their seeing any flaws in the outfit. No one wants to be sprayed by a skunk, let alone a big one capable of producing copious amounts of its malodorous chemicals. The ears, of course, were different; much smaller than mine. Jenny made me a black mask that covered my eyes as well as the top of my head out of some stretchy, black material she had scavenged, sort of a modified balaclava like a pirate might wear. She cleverly had sewn in a couple of tiny skunk-like ears into the top. The mask had the added benefit of being tight enough that it pressed my ears flat against my head to complete the illusion. Next, we needed to get the color and the markings right. Skunk turned out to be one of the easiest transformations. First, I bathed my entire body in black dye; a messy job indeed, but it converted me almost instantly to all black. In this state, we also created outfit number three: a pure black cat. Conversion to skunk from feline was easy. She back-brushed my tail to make it fluffier — like an out of control eighties hairdo — and held the fur in place with enough hairspray to make a small hole in the ozone layer. Then with two swift brushstrokes of white paint from the top of my head and down my back, and one little white line between my eyes and down my nose, I had yet another outfit: skunk.

We both stood there looking in the mirror admiring our work. "You look amazingly just like a skunk," a note of disbelief was in her voice. "I mean I thought it would work . . . but this is really good; quick too. I think we would only need about 30 minutes or less to get you into costume. Well, let's get you cleaned up and work on the next one. It might take you a while to wash all of that dye out of your fur." Jenny started scribbling in the notebook where she was keeping all the information on how to recreate each of my looks.

My eyes were still fixed on the mirror as I turned around and admired my appearance. Skunks were pretty quiet, so as long as I kept my mouth shut and moved in a skunk-like fashion, I should be able to fool just about anyone. I was about to head for the shower and multiple shampoos when a thought crossed my mind. "Hey Jenny, just wait a minute. I want to try something out." I was shouting to her over my shoulder as I headed for the exit, dashing outside and into the dusky evening. It was a little after the dinner hour and I had thought of a brilliant plan to put my costume to the test. I headed straight toward the badger burrow and burst through the door into the main living chamber. My sudden entrance caught the family of badgers by surprise and I noticed my old friends Kevin and Mark paralyzed with fear, staring at the skunk that had just barged into their family home. As I turned around and raised my tail, time seemed to slow down as the badgers fell over one another in a mad scramble to head for the tunnels, to the safety of the deepest parts of the burrow.

Unfortunately, there was one part of the skunk impression that I could not duplicate, not that any of the badgers were aware of that fact. However, I had been eating brussels sprouts for lunch at Jenny's place that day, and while unable to replace the skunk's spray, I did manage to crop dust the entire living area and make a hasty retreat before anyone knew what happened. Good times.

Jenny was waiting for me at the entrance as I scrambled back to her place. "Where did you go?" she asked, clearly a bit confused as to what was going on.

"Just a little test of the skunk disguise, a resounding success by the way!" I headed back inside quickly, a precaution in case a few angry badgers might be closing in from behind. A long, hot shower would soon hide the evidence of my crime and wash away any of my worries.

The next day we started working on costume number five: Mitzy or Lulu. Even we were not sure which one I was. Jenny had spent the entire day attaching a hair weave to my entire body. Prosthetic ears were used to enlarge my own and these were attached to my head with bobby pins. Another grey mask was made with the addition of a prosthetic that would lie on the bridge of my nose and hang over to create the illusion of a larger and fluffier mouth. Long hair extensions came down from the top of my forehead, over my eyes, and hid the mask's edges. We folded my tail in half and slid it into a sock that Jenny had made from the same hair she weaved into my body. This approximated the length and look of the Terriers tails. Two pairs of mittens concealed my hands and turned them into paws.

My legs were considerably longer than the dogs' were, so I learned to hunch my shoulders in such a way that made them appear shorter. It might not have worked if it was not for the long hair attached to the side of my body that hid my unusual walking stance. The sounds were the last details to perfect. The growls came naturally but the yips and barks were a little more difficult. I was confident that they would come with practice. *After all, if I could speak cat, how hard could dog be?*

Jenny held up some drawings of Mitzy and Lulu. "Yes, that looks right. I think we've got it. Took a long time, but I think it would fool Mitzy herself! Or Lulu?" She got distracted as her attention focused again on comparing me to the drawn images, trying to see any differences between the two. "I think we should put this disguise to the test. What would you say to a little adventure tonight?" Jenny gave me a mischievous look and a coy smile. "You might even find something good for us to eat other than brussels sprouts." With that Jenny and I got to making a plan for a caper at the Asters'.

CHAPTER 18

The Sampsons

JOHN SAMPSON WAS A VERY likable man. He was tall, with dark hair and an infectious smile. Not that he was unusually handsome — just likable. In general, he had a positive outlook on the world and could usually find the upside to most of the things that happened in his life.

For example, when he was younger, he once worked at a grocery store stocking shelves. The hours were long, and the pay was minimal, but he worked hard and tried to find ways to enjoy what he was doing. If the task was unpleasant, he would at least find pleasure in talking to the people he was working with. If there were no people to talk to, he would take satisfaction from doing the job well, no matter how menial it was. It was this general attitude, and his ability to radiate a sense of calmness in all situations that people were drawn to.

Not that everything always worked out for John. Some people would see his gentle demeanor and find fault, concluding that he was a little too easygoing. They would say that he was a slacker, or disorganized, or more interested in talking to people and joking around than doing his work; as if to imply that in some way working yourself into a frenzy over every little thing in life was the only way to show that you were hard working or passionate about what you were doing. While he tried his best to avoid problems with the type of personality that objected to his calm and patient approach to life, time and again it appeared they were especially interested in seeking out conflict with him.

John's supervisor at the grocery store was just such a person. Stuart J. Bonner. Stuart considered himself to be smart and knowledgeable. Mention something in the news, and off he would go with a string of facts and opinions, not that anyone had asked. It was obvious that Stuart spent most of his time absorbed in the day-to-day details of life, learning as many obscure facts and trivial details as he could fill his head with. In his mind, this was what was amazing about him, the thing that set him apart from other people. While he was great with obscure facts, the ability to interact socially was always a challenge for him. The fact that most of his relationships were complicated — even with his friends and family — just puzzled him even more. Deep down he could sense that even the people he thought of as his friends were just tolerating him most of the time.

One of the sources of Stuart's frustration was the gap between how he perceived himself and the reality of how others saw him, a common frustration to anyone in any kind of relationship, be it workmates, friends, or even marriage mates. The greater the gaps between those perceptions, the more strained relationships become, and the more frustrated both of the parties feel. In Stuart's mind, he was intelligent, driven, and deserving of respect from all the people around him. He could never understand why everyone else just did not see him the same way.

In his role as department supervisor at the local grocery store, Stuart was high-strung and demanding of those around him. In small glances, his superiors would see those qualities and reward him with praise and promotion, much to the chagrin of those forced to work under him. When he was promoted to assistant manager, it was as if someone finally confirmed his own opinion of himself. He felt like a king and acted accordingly. He seemed to completely forget the fact that his kingdom was just the local grocery store.

When John came to work at the store, there was just something about his easygoing approach to life that irritated Stuart to no end. *Why do people so easily give John the respect that I am so deserving of? Can they not see the same flaws in him that I see so clearly?* As with most of his relationships, he was unaware of his role in the problem, so his frustrations manifested outwardly. With this bias, he often singled out John to be the focus of his attention and the recipient of his animosity.

As John watched Stuart and his treatment of the other staff, along with his misplaced aggression towards him, it boggled his mind that someone decided this man should be the manager of anything. Apparently, this kind of behavior is what some consider to be leadership. Leadership to John was always more about what you do than what you say; inspire people to follow your example, rather than crack the whip as a taskmaster and shout the loudest, demeaning people like they were slaves. *Maybe I got it all wrong? Is this what is needed to get ahead in life, act like an arrogant tyrant, stepping on anyone you can to get ahead?*

It was after one particular conversation with Stuart that John came to some realizations about life and interacting with people that he was not particularly drawn to. After an unusually frustrating day, he found himself in the breakroom sitting across from the one person he least wanted to be around — a certain uptight assistant manager. His first instinct was to avoid eye contact and stare at his food while he consumed it as fast as possible. Something about that approach bothered him a little, and he stopped and took a long look at the annoying little man sitting in front of him. As he looked at him, he tried to see past his feelings of irritation and annoyance, set aside his prejudicial perceptions of the man, and look beyond the mask that low self-esteem and a frustrating life had placed upon the personality of Stuart J. Bonner.

As he scrutinized the *person* that was sitting across the table in front of him, he noticed something he had never seen before. A little sadness showed upon his face and in his eyes. *Where did that come from?* He had looked at his face a hundred times before, maybe a thousand times. It was then that he realized that he had never made much of an effort to get to know the man at all. *Could it be that there is more to him than I realized? Have I been so blinded by my feelings of irritation towards the man that I never really gave him a chance?* John came to the realization that, while this man did himself no favors, Stuart's annoying behavior was not the issue. The real question came down to what kind of man he wanted to be rather than the traits of the man that was sitting in front of him.

"Stuart, are you alright? You look a little down today. How is everything?" It was surprisingly hard to get the words out. *Why is asking such a simple question such a struggle?* He realized that what made it so difficult was that he had to trust his instinct that something was off in the first place. Next, he had to overcome the desire to not say anything at all, which was by far the easiest course of action. The voice inside his head was steering him to that conclusion as he struggled with the thought that he had probably just misread the look upon Stuart's face. It is so much easier to do nothing than to take a risk and make the effort to reach out to people. Finally, he had to prepare himself for an unknown response from an unpredictable man.

Bracing himself for the worst, a surprising thing happened. Caught off guard by someone showing a genuine personal interest in him, Stuart's face softened, and he replied in a low, sheepish voice. "Well, actually this has been a bad week. My wife and I have been having some problems for a while now. At the start of the week she went to stay with her mother for a few days . . ." The more Stuart spoke, the more he opened up and starting sharing details of his private life. It was like he was talking to the first person ever to express some interest in him as a human being. The words just came tumbling out of him and the more he spoke, the more John could see the influences that drove some of Stuart's actions and behaviors. The feelings of annoyance and irritation toward the man were being replaced by sympathy and compassion.

It was then that John realized he did not want to spend his life exasperated and resentful towards the people around him or let them decide if he would be happy that day or not. No matter how other people behaved, or even how they treated him, he would try to look beyond that and see the person for who they are. Instead of dismissing people, he would try to take a personal interest in them to help him understand the motivations behind their actions. Maybe he would learn that their behavior was being driven by family or social problems like in his recent encounter with Stuart. He thought of the many people he knew that had childhoods that would have messed anyone up. A lot of people are hiding their insecurity behind masks of aggression and bravado. It is also true that some people are just jerks no matter what you do or how much you reach out to them. In the end, John decided that it is worth the effort to reach out to people, even if there is the possibility that the other person will not respond favorably. No matter what others did, John could find contentment in being the kind of person he wanted to be.

It was this quiet confidence that Elizabeth Morales fell in love with. They met each other through mutual friends. John had started working for the fire department, and at the time Elizabeth was working as a nurse. They found conversation easy and made each other laugh. They dated, married soon after, and were eager to start their life together. They dreamed of traveling the world and exploring wonders they had only seen in pictures. That dream came to a sudden end when Elizabeth became pregnant with their first child. Life settled into the familiar pattern of work, cleaning, and keeping the kids entertained.

Even with children coming along earlier than they had planned, John and Elizabeth had a good life together. The ups and downs that they experienced were usually from external factors: parents with health problems, money getting tight when everything broke and needed to be repaired at the same time, and raising children which could be both joyful and maddening. Through it all, they always loved to be together.

So much of our time is spent in the banal cores of day-to-day living. If you can find someone whose companionship you enjoy when you are grocery shopping, cleaning the house and running errands, you have found a good thing. If that person can make you smile and laugh when you get a flat tire, or when you have to spend a few thousand dollars you don't have on something that you can't do without — if you are lucky enough to find that person — you should probably marry them.

John and Elizabeth worked hard to maintain their relationship and their friendship as they experienced all that life had to throw at them. They raised both their children, cared for Elizabeth's mom when she got sick with cancer and dealt with the death of both of Elizabeth's parents, and the ensuing grief that follows. Throughout it all, they managed to deal with problems between them quickly, to make sure to leave no fertile soil for the weeds of bitterness and resentment to grow. They went to great lengths to cultivate the love they shared and to firmly implant in their innermost thoughts and their daily speech all of the things they genuinely appreciated about each another.

They were just starting to get excited about planning the post-children phase of life when Elizabeth started feeling unwell. She had been more tired than usual and had been sleeping more than what was normal for her. Occasionally she would feel nauseous, but she just figured she was fighting the flu or something. When she started vomiting, she knew something was not right. The next morning, she made an appointment with the doctor, but she did not tell John as she did not want to worry him unnecessarily. Still, she had a nagging feeling the something was very wrong. Her thoughts flashed back to her mother, and the many long hours she had spent watching her suffer through chemotherapy and eventually wasting away until all that remained was a mere shell of the woman who had raised her.

The diagnosis from the doctor was something she was not prepared for. "You're pregnant," he stated bluntly, "about seven weeks now." It would have almost been less shocking to Elizabeth to hear that is was cancer.

"Pregnant? How? I don't understand?" she could hardly get the words out of her mouth, nervously fumbling with the open back of the thin, flimsy gown they had given her to wear for the examination.

"Well as to the how, I am sure if you think about it you can figure it out. You are not the first woman to get pregnant in her forties and probably won't be the last. We will set you up with a referral to an OBGYN because I think the one you had for your last pregnancy has probably retired by now. I will do some research on who might be a good fit for someone of your age and have my nurse give you a call." With that, the doctor turned and left her in shock, cold, and alone in the examination room.

The arrival of the new baby meant some adjustments for John and Elizabeth. After years of saving, they were almost ready to start planning the trip they had wanted to take before the children arrived. John's parents were willing to come and keep an eye on the house and the older children. Elizabeth had been adding to the scrapbook of Europe she had started when they were first married. Pictures of the Eiffel tower and the Matterhorn dotted its pages, along with numerous other places they were planning to visit. Now the money that was once earmarked to celebrate the next phase of their life went to all the expenses that come with a new baby. New clothes, a car seat, and diapers galore were the replacement for croissants, fondue, and copious amounts of fine French wine.

Seven months later the new baby came along right on schedule. They named the baby Sofia, after Elizabeth's grandmother. She had emigrated from Mexico when she was a young woman and had a big influence on Elizabeth's life growing up. She had passed away a few years before the baby was born, so in naming her after her grandmother, Elizabeth felt that it was a fitting tribute.

They converted John's office, which had previously been the oldest daughter's bedroom, back into a nursery. As an office, the room had been painted a bright sunny yellow and the large window allowed light to fill the room. The need new parents have to convert everything in baby's room to pink or blue had long since faded for the couple, along with the energy of their youth, so they decided to leave the yellow walls as they were. Elizabeth put the new crib in the corner, added new curtains, and decorated the room with stickers and pictures of forest animals. A few stuffed toys on the shelves and a changing table under the window, and they were ready for the arrival of the new daughter.

The room always tended to be on the warm side, but with the window open, fresh, cool air was allowed to flow in. Elizabeth always joked that they were going to be raising a mountain girl who will want to live outside her whole life with the window open all the time, but it stayed open anyway. John believed in the fresh air, and he could have sworn that Sofia liked to hear the sounds of nature at night.

CHAPTER 19

The Asters' Home

IT WAS WELL AFTER SUNSET when we arrived at the Asters' home. We had made our plan to scout the house, a quick in and out, hopefully without even seeing any of the humans. We set a signal between us; in the event of danger, or if one of us needed help, we would shriek like a crow as loud as we could. If I called, it meant Jenny had to come to my aid. If she called, it meant danger was imminent. If an actual crow cawed, well I am not sure what that would mean, but I am sure it would scare me nonetheless. No plan is perfect. Content that we were as ready as we could be, Jenny and I took up a position overlooking the back yard and the azalea bushes that lined the fence. Although well-concealed by the bushes to anyone who may have been in the back yard, the hole that Mitzy and Lulu had dug was obvious from our side of the fence. We hunkered down and quietly waited for the two little dogs to emerge, knowing they would be heading out into the forest for a night of adventure.

Mitzy and Lulu appeared on schedule and immediately headed out into the ravine, unaware that we had been watching, waiting for this opportunity. I wondered if maybe there were a few squirrels that were still out and about at this time of night that they could go nuts on. Jenny gave me a nudge and I headed in to do my reconnaissance of the Asters' yard and home. Sliding under the fence in my terrier costume was more difficult than I imagined, and a few of my weaves got caught in the cracks in the wood as I squeezed through. I turned back to see far too many strands of my 'fur' dangling from the bottom of the fence boards. I hoped that it did not affect the overall believability of my look as a terrier. The point was to avoid attention, and a bald spot on the back of their beloved pet would surely not help me go incognito. Hoping that there was only minimal damage, I took a quick and cautious look around the yard and then proceeded to make my way towards the doggy door.

As I approached the house I was suddenly hit with a blinding light. Out of instinct, I stood up on my hind legs and used my hands to shield my eyes from the light. I thought for sure the lights meant that someone in the house had seen me, so I stood there motionless, waiting to see if I would have to bid a hasty retreat in the event that one of the humans emerged with a net or some other diabolical anti-raccoon device. After standing motionless for about 30 seconds, the lights went out and the yard went dark again. No human was seen, and the house was as quiet as ever. It was only then, as I lowered my hands from my eyes, that I realized that if someone had investigated, they would have seen their pet standing in a very unusual position. Dogs do not stand on their hind legs and cover their eyes with the backs of their paws. *A dead giveaway that you're a raccoon Gary!* I would have to learn — especially in stressful situations — to keep up the behaviors of the animals I was impersonating. Otherwise, it would not matter how good my costume was.

I took a few more steps towards the house, and the lights turned on again. This time I was a little more prepared and managed to keep my feet on the ground. Again, after about 30 seconds, the light turned off without the appearance of any human. *I think it's responding to my movement.* I started walking again, and this time when the lights turned on, instead of freezing in place, I continued on until I reached the entrance. The lights turned off again, and with everything still quiet, I made my entrance into the Asters' home.

Their place was quite different from Mrs. Abrams', albeit this was only the second human home I had ever seen the inside of. I'm not sure if

I was expecting them to all look the same; in my world, a porcupine's home is not much different than a possum's or a rabbit's. The Asters' abode was much larger and more open in its layout. From where I entered the kitchen area, I felt as if I could see most of the house. To my left there was a large living room with a fireplace; a few coals still glowed on the hearth. The main entrance was directly in front of me, with a beautiful white marble floor and an ornate chandelier hanging from the vaulted ceiling. To my right, past the kitchen area, a long hallway led to the bedrooms and the other areas of the house. As I could see so much of the home from just inside the door, I realized this meant I was also clearly visible to anyone moving around in the house. Suddenly I felt very exposed. If something went wrong this time, there was no place to hide.

It had appeared that the Asters had entertained guests earlier in the evening. Little plates with bits of food left on them sat upon the small tables in the living area. Wine glasses and half-empty water bottles could be seen strewn about on many of the horizontal surfaces. Dishes were piled up in the kitchen sink and it looked like the decision had been made to worry about the cleanup in the morning.

Having learned that the safest time to explore was immediately after my doppelganger had exited, I decided to start by checking out the hallway off the kitchen that led to the bedrooms. The hallway was long, covered by a soft cream-colored carpet which contributed to the silence of my stealthy exploration. In addition to the bedrooms, I discovered a large office with a wooden desk and a library's worth of books along the walls. Comfortable leather furniture and forest green walls completed the look. Another room contained a home theater, with a half dozen over-sized chairs pointing at the large screen on the wall. So many warm and cozy places to nap; I envied the two terriers. I took a survey of the bedrooms. Fortunately, the door to Mr. and Mrs. Aster's room was closed but not latched, a by-product of living with pets I imagine, so with just a little push I got a clear view of the sleeping couple. In one of the other bedrooms I could hear the soft noises of other humans rolling around in their bed. This door was completely closed, and I was content to just give a short listen and then keep on searching. They were probably party guests that were spending the night.

After making a good mental map of the hallway and its adjacent rooms, I headed back to the kitchen and living area, and I wondered what I could do to reward myself for my bravery up to this point before heading back out into the yard. The temptation of the leftovers in the living area had been percolating in my mind from the moment I saw them.

I climbed up on to the sofa in the living room and sniffed around at the remains on the plates. Some half-eaten cake soon became wholly eaten. Bits of cheese and crackers were gleefully hoovered up by yours truly. The crowning jewel came when I discovered an appetizer platter on the coffee table, full of nature's greatest miracle — cocktail wieners. I climbed on to the coffee table and began wantonly wolfing down the wieners. The tiny sausages exploded in my mouth with bursts of fat and flavor. Conveniently a little wine had been left in a glass next to the snacks and my meal was complete. *Cocktail weenies — who can resist?*

Upon finishing my meal, I knew I had to bring Jenny some bounty from the mission and looked around for something to grab. The cocktail weenies would have been perfectly portable, but they had somehow completely disappeared. Heading into the kitchen, I started to open a few of the lower cabinets. The first one held pots and pans. The next cabinet under the sink was filled with only chemicals and cleaning solutions. *Pass.* I was almost about to give up when I caught a whiff of something from the large gleaming metal box in the corner of the kitchen. This box was different from the other cabinet doors that were so easy to open. I clawed and pulled at the corner, but nothing happened. *What made this human box different from any other box?* Seeing a separation that ran down the center, I reached my hands under the bottom in the middle and pulled with all my might. The doors swung open with a loud smash of bottles and jars clanging into one another. Bright light hit me like I was suddenly starring in a Broadway play. Feeling naked and exposed I couldn't move. Bathed in the light from the silver box, I thought for sure my time was up and I would be discovered as a thieving imposter. As the minutes passed, I listened anxiously for the footfalls of some angry Asters, but nothing happened. The house remained silent. As the fear started to ebb out of me and movement returned to my limbs, I turned my attention to the illuminated layers of food and various bottles and containers that were displayed before me.

Vegetables and fruit occupied the lower shelves. Taller containers occupied the upper shelves. I sniffed the air. *Is that cream?* The top shelf became the focus of my attention, and finding a pathway up dominated my thoughts. The shelves themselves formed a ladder of sorts. The plastic material made it difficult for my fingers to dig into, but metal supports and spaces between the plastic and glass shelving aided my ascent. As I clambered up to the first level, standing in front of the vegetable crisper, the smells of meat and cheese filled my nostrils. It was definitely coming from the drawer marked *deli*. I pawed and clawed at the plastic drawer, eager to ravage the contents inside. Despite all my best attempts, they remained safely encased in their artificial cocoon. Then I remembered that so far, most of the human containers responded better to a pull than a push. I reached my fingers under the lip of the drawer and pulled it towards me. The drawer slid open easily and I was overwhelmed with the delicious, delectable aromas that were emanating from it.

I grabbed at packages of cheese and meat and started to feast on the deli drawer's contents. When I could eat no more, I grabbed a comical amount of food — as much of the drawer's contents as I could carry — and headed out of the house. Due to the quantity of my loot, I had to stuff the food through the doggy door first, and then follow behind. *Everything is going so smoothly.* But then, just as I gathered all the food up in my arms again, I heard the urgent sound of a crow cawing from beyond the fence.

I froze, afraid and unsure of the source of the danger. If Mitzy and Lulu were coming back into the yard I was sunk. I doubted my disguise would fool either of them for even a second; animals are much more perceptive than humans, and with there being two of them, I did not think that I had any chance to outrun them both. I would be lucky to escape with my hide, let alone any of my bounty. I cautiously put my stolen goods down on a patio chair, and stared out into the darkness, bracing myself for the onslaught to come. It only took a few moments to realize that the danger was not coming from the forest but from behind me. A light had turned on in the kitchen and the Asters' guest, after grabbing himself a beer, was opening the patio door and coming outside into the back yard. Unsure if he had seen me or not, I decided it would be best not to get caught with my loot, so I put some space between myself and the cold cuts.

The man came outside and spotted me right away. "Here pup, come here, shhhh, no need to bark little guy, shhhh." He was apparently more afraid of me making noise and waking up the house than he was genuinely interested in having me come over to him, and I felt like I had control of the situation. If he had appeared suspicious of me or had looked at me too intently, I would have gone into a fierce and frenzied barking freak-out. I was sure he would retreat or at least be distracted enough that it would provide me ample opportunity to escape. Feeling confident, I trotted over to the man to see if I could get a better look at him. "That's it girl, come here. Which one of those mutts are you? Mitzy or Lulu? Where is the other one?" From the tone in his voice, it was clear he was not overly fond of the troublesome canines. "That's it you spoiled brat. No need to raise the alarm. You know me. Just slipping out for a late-night brewski. Let's keep this our little secret." There was an implied wink in the tone of his voice.

I was not sure if it was the darkness or the effects of the beer on top of the evening's libations, but he appeared to be completely unaware of the fact that I might be anyone other than Mitzy or Lulu. He leaned up against the side of the house and tipped his bottle skyward to finish off his drink. "Well, that's it for me pup. You coming back inside?" He held the door open for me to follow. Too risky I thought. I gave gruff little growl and he soon got the idea. "Suit yourself," he said as he slid the door closed behind him. A minute later the light inside the house went out and I headed over to the patio chair where I had left my prize. Even the automatic lights would not be a problem as they would just assume it was the dogs setting them off. Confidently, I strode to the patio chair I had left the snacks on, and scooping everything up, I ran across the lawn, fully illuminated and in plain sight. When I reached the fence, I put everything in the tunnel under the fence and pushed my way through, food and all. Putting a safe distance between us and the Asters, Jenny and I celebrated our latest success by digging into some of the tasty snacks I had managed to rescue. Who knew rabbits liked deli meat?

CHAPTER 20

Multiple Identities

AFTER COMPLETING THREE DIFFERENT TRIAL runs, in three different outfits, we were both feeling confident that the plan was going to work. We received additional confirmation that the skunk identity had been a success when the day after my crop-dusting foray, the entire badger family spent the morning handing out a sketch, asking if anyone knew this particular stinker. When they came knocking at Jenny's door, we did our best to seem confused and shocked by the whole disturbing incident. Even though Jenny quickly pieced together who the real culprit was, she played the part well enough that the badgers moved on with their search without suspecting my involvement. We also agreed that if we used the skunk identity again, we had to make sure the white markings were painted on in a pattern that was sufficiently different so that the badgers would not recognize me as their emanating invader.

In the end, after all of our hard work and Jenny's creative solutions to numerous costume challenges — including washing my fur more times in a few days than I had in my entire life — we came up with three lists of the animals that I could realistically impersonate:

<u>Animals that will be easy to impersonate — minimal alteration and recovery time:</u>

Mr. Pickles (Mask, minimal color changes)
Baby Lynx (Special boots, tuft extensions, mask)

Porcupine (Quill body suit, fake nose)

Animals to impersonate which require time and advanced preparation:

Mitzy and Lulu (Extensive hair weaves, tail prosthesis)
Skunk (Full dye job — black and white paint for stripes, mask with ears)
Rabbit (Ear extensions, fur dye, slight whisker trim, tail tuck, fake tail attachment)
Young Fox (Orange dye, white paint for markings, extreme puff job for tail)

Animals to impersonate which require significant alteration and recovery time:

(Mostly to allow things to grow back)
Possum (Tail needs to be shaved)
Badger (Boots, mask, dyeing, striping, whisker removal)
Hairless Cat (Complete shave of all fur, whisker removal)

The list was long and included many more animals than I had thought possible. We also made a list of the local animals we could not imitate. Squirrels, chipmunks, snakes, and any of the local birds were just too difficult. We even thought of a human baby, but the hairless ears on the side of the head was just too big of an obstacle to overcome. Even if we were able to make the appearance believable, it might upset the humans too much to see baby climbing up the side of a house or rummaging in the trash cans. The other animals we eliminated were bears, wolves, and deer. Their larger sizes made it impossible for us to put together a reasonable impersonation without having considerably more time and resources to work with.

We had also come to realize that to really sell an impression, imitating the sounds and movements of the animal was as important as the costume, if not more so. Being disguised as a cat was one thing, but if I let out a good meow and licked my fur convincingly, no one would even take a second look, even if the costume wasn't perfect. I picked up most of the behaviors without too much trouble, but it would always be something I would have to study and then practice to perfection. The success and snacks of my recent sojourns provided me with plenty of motivation to continue to work on my newfound skills.

"With some of these animals, I am going to require time to collect the raw materials we need, and then to turn them into garments you can use. The porcupine impression, for example, I wonder how I'm going to get a full set of quills to make your suit. I would almost need to hogtie and shave one of them bald . . ." Jenny's voice trailed off in thought as she continued to make sketches on the whiteboard. The scary thing was, I couldn't tell if she was serious about the hog-tying or not.

With most of the work done and all the plausible ideas explored, I wondered aloud about what we should do next. "I have a family that I would like you to meet," Jenny replied. "We're going to test out your new skills. Come on let's go!" Jenny hopped away and headed out the door. I knew better than to try and dissuade her when she was on a mission.

She led us out deeper into the forest. We scampered under the trees and bushes for about ten minutes until we approached a large, stately elm tree. In front of the tree, a mass rose from the forest floor. Rocks and soil had built up there and created a mound a few feet higher than the rest of the terrain. Various shrubs and ferns had grown up, around, and over the little hill. Someone had dug an opening at the base of the mound, and this was serving as the entrance to a home.

"Hello?" Jenny called into the tunnel opening. "Gwendolyn, are you home? It's me, Jenny!" After a minute or two, we could hear shuffling in the tunnel as someone approached. When Gwendolyn finally appeared, her eyes were blinking as she adjusted to the light of the outside world. Jenny gave her a half embrace (which is about all you can do with a porcupine). "How is your daughter doing? Is she feeling any better? Does she still have the cough?"

You could hear the sadness in the mother porcupine's voice as she replied, "I'm afraid she has gotten worse Jenny. She can't stop with the coughing and she has had a fever for the last day and a half. Come inside and take a look for yourself. Bring your friend with you," she said as she turned around to start back down the tunnel.

We emerged into the stale air of the porcupine family's dimly lit den. The home was laid out in an L shape, with a few side chambers that were used as bedrooms. There was a kitchen off to one side. Nuts and seeds were neatly stacked in the corner. A few of the sleeping areas had been built up with leaves and anything else soft that the forest could supply. One of the beds had a soft, cloth blanket lining a little hollow of a sleeping area. It looked like something that had blown off a clothesline on a particularly windy day and had been repurposed to make a comfy sleeping spot. From the middle of the blanket bed, I could hear a persistent, nagging cough coming from a little girl.

"Here she is Jenny, here is Emma. The other children are out with their father foraging. Take a look at her and see what you think." Jenny went over to the tiny little porcupine and put her paw on her forehead.

"She's burning up Gwen. Let me have a listen to her chest." They propped Emma up so that Jenny could lower an ear to her side and listen. "Just breathe as deeply as you can Emma. Try not to cough." Jenny listened intently to the little porcupine's breathing. She could hear a distinctive rattle inside her lungs each time she tried to draw a breath. She laid Emma down again and settled her into a comfortable position. "Now just get some rest, Emma, you'll be feeling better soon." Jenny tried to sound reassuring, but you could hear the concern in her voice.

She turned to the girl's mother. "I'm afraid she's got pneumonia Gwen, no doubt about it. Have you been giving her any kind of medicine?"

Gwendolyn fussed over her ailing little daughter as she replied, "we had her chewing on some birch bark for the pain, but that's all we have. Oh Jenny, I'm so worried about her and not sure what I should do."

Jenny looked the anxious porcupine in the eye and made a promise. "Don't worry Gwen. We'll go get some medicine for Emma and hurry back here as soon as we can." With that Jenny motioned to me that it was time to leave and we quickly headed out the door

CHAPTER 21

The Mallard Family

IT HAD BEEN A DAY or two since Max and Jonathan had discovered the bodies of the two dead possums. The crime was particularly disturbing, and the image of the two bloated bodies weighed upon Max's mind ever since he had seen them on that sandbar. The thing that bothered Max's clever fox brain was that usually, this level of violence came with a clear motive. This time there was no apparent explanation for the crime. If hunger were the driving force, the bodies would have been consumed to some extent. Humans tend to trap or kill and then dispose of the carcasses in the garbage or by fire, not by tossing them in a creek. As he eliminated many of the usual catalysts, Max was beginning to wonder if this could be an act of pure malevolence; someone who took pleasure in the act, rather than someone who killed for gain or to accomplish a specific purpose. The thought of that kind of killer loose in the woods sent a cold shiver down his spine.

Instead of focusing on the little evidence they had, Max decided to mull over what the profile of a perpetrator of this kind of crime would be. That might help narrow down his search. It could be human. They were known to be violent against animals at times. They were also constantly thinking of new ways to control nature, which usually meant inventing an infinite variety of devices and methods to terminate animals. It would not be the work of your usual human though. It would have to be someone with an intent to destroy that goes far beyond the protection of a few fruits and vegetables. To be capable of disposing of the bodies so callously, it would have to be an act of hatred towards animals. Or perhaps the killer himself was consumed by anger and hatred, and the possums just happened to be in the wrong place at the wrong time.

The other possibility Max considered is that this was animal on animal violence. That line of reasoning led him to consider some dark possibilities. Unlike humans, animal motives were usually simple. Food, shelter, and mating were common denominators. He had already ruled out hunger as a motive due to the condition of the bodies. *Mating?* It is a powerful driver of animal behavior to be sure. What could be gained by killing both the male and the female of the possum family? Surely a rival male would have killed just the husband, to take the wife as his own. *Why kill them both? Whose purpose would that serve?* Max was considering the possibility that shelter was a factor when Jonathan came dashing in. "There has been another incident; another family has been found dead! Come quickly, there is no time to waste!" With that, Jonathan bounded off and Max had to hustle to keep up with his diminutive friend.

The creek that ran down through the bottom of the ravine leveled off at a flat spot between the two hillsides, forming a large pool. The depth of the pond was never more than nine or ten feet at its deepest point, but it was a haven for the birds and animals in the area. The trees were far enough away from the water's edge that if you looked heavenward, you could see the forest canopy open up and reveal a patch of blue sky. The light that streamed down to the forest floor allowed for a wide variety of plants that could not have survived in the more shaded parts of the ravine. The ensuing oasis became home to a wide variety of creatures. Even the cranes would swoop down from time to time to walk the pond and see what fish or amphibians they could make a meal of. A variety of waterfowl had built nests in the cattails and rushes that lined the edges of the little pond.

It was to this location that Jonathan had led Max, with a couple of mallard ducks being the focus of attention. The warm spring had brought with it an early mating season for the ducks and other birds that made the pond their home. Good weather and plentiful food meant some especially dazzling colors on the part of the drake. Who can resist the glorious luster of a shiny green head? Not the female duck, that was for sure. A successful mating of the pair had resulted in the young hen building a fine nest in among the cattails. She had laid a dozen or so eggs in the nest and had attended to them faithfully.

As Max and Jonathan arrived to survey the gruesome scene, they found that the hen and the drake had both been murdered. Someone had chewed through both their necks leaving behind two headless bodies. Max surmised that the male had been done in first. His body lay two to three feet away from the nest. No doubt he had charged at the attacker in an attempt to save his mate and offspring. Once the drake had been eliminated, the attacker had turned its attention to the hen. She had bravely remained on the eggs that she was incubating, no doubt hissing and flapping, trying to do everything she could to defend them from the brutal attacker without abandoning her unhatched ducklings. Alas, she too was overcome by her assailant and relieved of her head.

Max surveyed the area around the crime scene and then proceeded with his examination of the bodies. After an uncomfortably long silence, he finally spoke to his chipmunk companion. "They were not eaten, despite the fact that their heads are missing. Even if the heads had been eaten, it would not have constituted a full meal for a creature powerful enough to overwhelm these two. Again, the crime appears to be more an act of violence rather than any of the usual motivations. Most disturbing indeed."

Jonathan had watched Max at the scene of many crimes. Granted, they were usually the 'who stole my winter stash of nuts?' type of crime, not the wanton butchery that was in front of them. In all the cases they had worked together, he had never seen Max as perplexed and unsettled as he was now. "Do you think it could be the work of the same person who attacked the possum family?" Jonathan asked. A slight quiver could be heard in his little chipmunk voice.

"Well, the motive is equally obscure in both of the cases, even though the method used in this killing was more of a direct attack than the previous one. That might have been due to the fact that the assailant knew he had nothing to fear from any counterattack. I can't rule out the possibility that these two events are linked." Max had made his statement with a somewhat reluctant tone; as if two murderers running around in the forest would have somehow been the preferable option. The more Max thought about the violent nature of the crimes — and now across at least two species — it seemed less and less likely that any attempt to expropriate real estate was the motive for either of these killings.

CHAPTER 22

The First Mission

THE FIRST MISSION HAD NOW become clear to Jenny. Somehow, we needed to get the medicine to cure little Emma. As Jenny and I headed back to her place to devise a plan, she was deep in thought. I knew that whenever Jenny got this quiet, it meant that the gears inside her mind were turning furiously.

When we arrived at Jenny's home, she immediately went into action heading straight to the whiteboard where we had written down our list of personas. She circled Mr. Pickle's name with a bright red marker. "This mission is urgent, and I don't think it's time to try something new. We know the Pickles disguise works; it will give us the best chance of a successful mission." She went over to the map where she had drawn Mrs. Abrams' home and property and started to draw arrows indicating all the known entrances. "That means the old lady's home is the target. You'll enter the home through the cat door." She drew a large red arrow pointing at the side door. She wrote the number one next to the arrow and wrote 'insertion point'. Under the heading 'Mission goals' she wrote: 1) Search the house for medication that could help Emma. 2) Steal any food that you can carry to help the porcupine family in their time of need. 3) Make a mental map of the home as you search.

"The mission is to look for medications that could help Emma. That is the primary goal. But we have never done any reconnaissance of the inside of the Abrams' place and this will be our best chance to learn what resources are inside that could help us in the future. Take a good look around if it is safe and try to remember as many details as possible." She spoke without the slightest hesitation or doubt as to the success of the plan. *Sure,* I thought to myself, *it is as easy as one, two, three.*

CHAPTER 23

Operation Abrams

OF COURSE, THE ACTUAL PLANNING was a little more complicated than that, but we worked out as many of the details as we possibly could that afternoon. We tried to account for every variable we could imagine.

Here is the gist of what we came up with: we would both wait in the bushes, downwind of the cat door. After Mr. Pickles had emerged for his nocturnal routine, I was to head to the door and enter the home. I would do a quick reconnaissance of the basement level first, as that area had the least escape routes and it would be safest to explore immediately after Pickles had left. Then I was to head up to the main floor and look for the bathroom, where hopefully I would be able to find medication for Emma. Antibiotics was the word Jenny made me repeat over and over. She even had me write it out on the whiteboard — like a kid writing lines in detention — to make sure I would recognize it when I saw it. We also spent hours practicing my movements and sounds, trying to perfect the imitation of our feline friend. The exit plan was this: push the cat flap once and wait for about five seconds. If there was danger outside Jenny would be watching and again start cawing like a crow signaling that I remain in the house. If I did not hear Jenny's warning call, five seconds later I would come out the cat flap and run to the bushes for safety. The perfect crime.

I had a nervous knot in my stomach as we sat there waiting that evening, staring at that cursed cat door, trying not to think of Johnny and all the other horrible things that could go wrong. Jenny had been primping and preening me for at least an hour, adjusting my fur, my mask, and touching up the dye she used to hide my raccoon markings. She had even painted something on my nose to make it more permanently pink this time. Apparently, the strawberry she used to color my nose on our first mission in the garden did not last, as I had licked it off in the first few seconds of the operation without even noticing. This time she muttered something about crushing up beetles and dared me to 'lick *this* off', as she fussed to cover up any black spots that were poking through.

As much as she tried to be positive, I could sense from Jenny a kind of nervous energy, and that was feeding my fear. She did not say anything specific, but the way she could not stop fiddling was a dead giveaway. I thought of bailing on the whole crazy thing but the image of little Emma, lying there so helpless in her bed, helped me to refocus my thoughts on the mission at hand.

We had surveyed the entire house from the outside before we took our position in the bushes. To help keep my mind from wandering, I ran through all the possible exit plans in my head. If the cat flap was blocked, the old lady's bedroom window was half-open. The screen could be ripped or chewed. I had noticed another window in the basement was slightly ajar. It might work, but it was the riskier choice due to the unknowns. *Would I have the strength to open it wide enough to get through, or the time to rip open the screen? Would that even be possible if I were being pursued by Mr. Pickles? Would it be a straight jump from the floor, or is there something in front of the window I could use to get on to the sill?* My thoughts were racing but I could feel everything coming into focus, like I was some kind of ninja. *Raccoon Ninja.* I liked the sound of that. *Rinja? No, not quite right. Nincoon? There it is. I am the night. I am Nincoon!* I looked over at Jenny with a confident smirk, about to share my awesome thought with her, when I caught myself. *Sounds awfully close to something else.* I could hear Jenny's sarcastic tone in my head. *"Nincoon?"* she would say, *"more like Nincoonpoop!" Ouch. Better not set her up with an easy one like that.* I averted my gaze just a moment before we would have made eye contact and then pretended that I did not see her staring back at me. *Better stick to thinking about emergency escape routes.*

We waited for what seemed like hours after the sun had set before there was finally movement at the cat door. Mr. Pickles, pushing his head out cautiously at first, took a long sniff of the air. *Strange. I didn't think of him as a cautious type. He struts around like he is the king of the world. I guess fear and insecurity are common to everyone.* After a couple of sniffs and partial openings, Mr. Pickles finally burst out the door and into the night. He went immediately into a defensive stance as his eyes darted back and forth. Somewhere my brain filed a note: *overconfidence is often used to conceal insecurity.* Maybe that would be of help sometime if I ended up in a confrontation with Mr. Pickles. After assuring himself that it was safe to proceed, Mr. Pickles headed out for his nightly routine. I knew from experience the circuit he usually took and that I had a couple of hours to complete my mission; plenty of time, unless something went wrong of course.

We gave Mr. Pickles a five-minute head start before I made my move for the door. I looked over at Jenny and had the terrifying thought that this could be the last time I ever saw her beautiful face. I wanted to tell her how much she meant to me but was afraid that by speaking I might reveal our position and put her in danger. I gazed at her face, inviting her eyes to look at mine one last time. When they finally met, my eyes said 'wish me luck and goodbye forever' all in one glance. There was a look of both hope and fear in her eyes, as she leaned into me, touching her head to mine. The warmth of her soft, white fur against mine gave me a momentary burst of courage, so I headed for the door before the feeling faded away.

I crept silently along the wall of the house, just as Johnny had done so many nights ago. The brick still radiated heat from the day's sun, and

I could feel the warmth emanating off the house as I snuck along the wall. All the practice with Jenny had paid off as I was moving much more cat-like without having to think about what every limb was doing. When I arrived at the cat door, I gave one last glimpse back toward the bushes and Jenny. I could not see her and felt a twinge of disappointment. But realizing that meant she was well-hidden and safe, I turned my attention to the door. I slowly pushed into the flap until it opened just enough that my nose was inside the house with the flap covering my face and eyes. My muscles tensed as I half expected some horrible creature to grab hold and drag me in. But the only thing to grab me was an over-whelming scent that filled my nostrils as I slowly drew the air in. The memories of decades of Mrs. Abrams' cooking and baking oozed out of the walls towards me. *Is that cinnamon?* I could have just sat there for hours sniffing at the air. But I had a mission to accomplish, so I pushed the rest of the way through the flap and into the house. Now standing in the front entrance, I could see a small set of stairs in front of me that led to the main floor. To my right, the stairs plunged into the darkness of the basement. Remembering the plan, I headed down the stairs and into the blackness.

Halfway down, the stairs turned to the left and then ended in a large open room. My eyes needed to adjust to the dark as the only light coming into the basement was from a streetlamp outside. The light filtered through some curtains to provide a dim glow in the room. I could see that there was wood paneling on all the walls and a green shag carpet on the floor. A large brown sectional couch was in the middle of the room with a mishmash of chairs that looked like they had been taken from a half dozen different living room sets over the years. Various bookshelves lined the opposite wall and there was an old-fashioned roll top desk in the corner. The whole room had a slightly musty smell, as you would expect in a carpeted basement. I made my way through the den to a hallway that led to a couple of bedrooms and a mechanical room that housed the furnace and the water heater. I made a mental map of the layout, took note of the bedroom that had the partially opened window, and made my way back to the stairs to explore the upper floors.

The stairs to the main floor led up to a large sitting room. It was clean and tidy with doilies on the coffee table and a couch and chair that were wrapped in plastic. The room looked fancy and dated at the same time and I got the impression that no one ever spent much time there.

A large opening in the wall led to a spacious hallway with the kitchen on the left and a dining room across from the kitchen on the right. There were two openings along the wall that served as entrances into the kitchen. My stomach rumbled a little thinking of all the things I might find in there. *Mission first, snacks later,* I reminded myself, not sure if it was my voice or Jenny's rattling around in my head. The dining room had a large antique table and chairs, and a hutch full of china and other dishes. *Nothing of interest here.*

Further down the hall past the kitchen was the main floor bathroom and another flight of stairs leading to the second floor. I headed into the bathroom, as Jenny said that would be the most likely place I would find the human medicines. The bathroom was small, with a blue porcelain sink and a matching toilet and tub. Green towels hung on racks against a backdrop of wallpaper with a large floral print. A linen closet door was partially open, and I gave it a swift search. There were towels, sheets, soap, shampoo; nothing that looked like medicine.

Below the sink, there was a cabinet with a set of double doors. Pushing and pulling I clawed away at the bottom of the door trying to figure how to get inside. Pulling appeared to be the way to go, so I grabbed the metal handle and gave it a tug. The door swung open and a strong smell of chemicals overwhelmed me. I could see various colored, plastic bottles and rags but nothing that looked like the small containers I was looking for. The bottles were all too big and the noxious odors were burning my nostrils. Closing the door, I decided to hop up on to the sink to have a look around. There was a bar of soap on one side, and a bottle with a pump on the top on the other side. I pushed down on the top of the bottle to see what would happen. Some kind of creamy substance came out and made a small pile on the blue porcelain sink. I hesitantly put my fingertips into the goo and then brought them up to my nose. *Smells nice, like flowers.* I gave my fingers a lick, which turned out to be a huge mistake. *Yuck!* I rapidly rubbed the rest of the cream into my hands, trying to get rid of the oily substance. As the cream slowly disappeared, being absorbed into my tiny hands, I couldn't help but notice how soft they were becoming.

The mirror in front of the sink protruded out of the wall. I caught a glimpse of my reflection in the mirror and my heart skipped a beat. Between the mask and the coloring on my nose, for an instant I did not recognize myself. Regaining my composure, I started to feel around the frame of the mirror. Something about it gave me the impression that it was covering over something, a compartment maybe. Feeling along the bottom, and remembering how I opened the lower cabinet, I gave it a strong pull. The mirror held, as if some force were trying to keep it closed. When it finally released, it swung open so violently that I had to catch myself from stumbling backward and falling off the sink. After I regained my balance, I refocused my attention on what was behind the open door. *A secret compartment!* My excitement grew as I carefully searched each shelf; ointment, cream, floss, paste — everything but the word antibiotic. It was crammed with lots of little jars and bottles, but not the one I was looking for. Disappointed at not finding what I wanted, I closed the secret mirrored door and jumped down on to the bathroom floor. *Maybe this was all a big mistake.* There was still time to check the second floor, to see if the medicine was there, but in my heart, I felt our chances were fading. Silently I made my way out of the bathroom and across the hall to the stairs that led up to the second level.

I started climbing the staircase, but to my chagrin, the old stairs were noisier than one would like when engaged in a stealth mission. Each step creaked and groaned under my weight, and each noise sent a hot flash of panic through my nervous system. I tried to tread as slowly and softly as possible, first in the middle of the steps, then along the sides, but the old house continued to moan like an arthritic senior getting up out of a chair. After a particularly loud screech from one of the looser boards, I became convinced that the old lady was about to wake up and at any moment she would suddenly appear at the top of the staircase to see what was happening. Muscles tensed and ears on alert, I listened intently for human footfalls on the floor above me and the sound of my inevitable doom. Standing motionless on the steps, afraid to move up or down out of fear of making any more noise, I waited for what seemed to be an eternity. As the minutes passed and the night remained still and quiet, my body relaxed, and my fear started to subside. The only sound I could hear in the distance was some heavy breathing and an occasional snort from Mrs. Abrams. Note to self: *Things always seem worse from my perspective. What fear and anxiety magnify in the mind goes largely unnoticed by others.*

There were three bedrooms and a bathroom on the second floor. I peeked into the two empty bedrooms. They looked as if they had not been disturbed for many years. Mrs. Abrams' bedroom was larger than the other two. I leaned my head past the door frame and listened for any danger. All I could hear was the rhythmic breathing of Mrs. Abrams as she slept. Entering the room, I paused to survey the scene. A large four-poster bed was in the middle of the room along the back wall with nightstands on each side. A large desk and dresser were on the opposite wall and numerous bottles and other items were on a little table beside the bed. I wondered if one of them might be the item I was looking for.

As quietly as I could, I crept alongside the bed to get a look at what was on the old lady's nightstand. My heart was pounding as the sound of her breathing grew louder the closer I got. When I reached the night-stand, it was a little higher than I expected. Standing on my hind legs I could just barely get my head over the top to take a look. I saw a glass of water, a hairbrush, and a few tubes of something. A white container that had been placed at the back of the nightstand caught my attention, and squinting my eyes, I attempted to get them to focus in the dark, enough so that I could read the writing on the label. *Ant* . . . I could just make out the first few letters on the bottle. Stretching out my arm, I tried care-fully to reach between the glass and the other bottles without knocking any of them over. I strained my arm to its limit, but the bottle remained out of reach of my little raccoon arms. *Now what should I do? This could be the medicine I have been looking for. Too far in to turn back now.* Feeling it was worth the risk, I jumped up onto the table. I would grab the medi-cine and run for the door before anyone knew what happened. *Cool as a cucumber. Stealthy as a cat. Scratch that. Stealthy as a Nincoon! No, we gave that up, didn't we? Stealthy as a raccoon? Could that be a thing? It would have to do.* I made my leap onto the nightstand and immediately knew I had misjudged the size of my landing area. The glass of water and the brush came crashing down onto the wood floor and made a terrible racket. I froze in place as Mrs. Abrams, roused by the noise, rolled over to face me. "Is that you Pickles?" the old lady said in a voice that was half-awake and half-asleep. I had to think fast.

"Merow" . . . *what were the other low rumbly sound cats made?* "Rrrrrrr, rrrrrrr". I tried my best.

"C'mere boy." Her hand was feeling around in the dark for what she assumed was Pickles. My mind was racing. *Should I head for the door? Stay where I am?* Mrs. Abrams started patting the bed beside her. "C'mere and sleep, boy. I'll scratch your ears for you." Out of instinct, I jumped down on the spot she had been patting. *Maybe this was a bad idea.* Her hand found my head and she started scratching my chin and ears. *Maybe this wasn't a bad idea.* "Now settle down and go to sleep boy," she said. Her hands did feel good, and for a few seconds I forgot where I was. Maybe if I played the part, she would fall back to sleep none the wiser. I curled up into a ball and snuggled against the old woman. I could feel the heat from her body and the warmth was making me sleepy. Her hand rested on my head and neck and I knew the only option I had was to wait her out, let her fall back asleep and then slip out and continue my mission. Sitting there waiting in the dark, next to a human who was the equivalent of a warm sunbeam, it became harder and harder to keep my eyes open. I was trying to wait until the old lady's breathing fell into the same pattern as I had heard before when I was coming up the stairs, but it was I who dozed off before Mrs. Abrams did.

The next thing I remembered was waking up in complete darkness. Forgetting for a second where I was, it took me a moment to regain my senses. Then a feeling of panic started to come over me as I remembered where I was. *How much time had passed? Was Mr. Pickles back in the house? Should I bolt for the exit?* Adrenaline had all of my senses back on full alert. My body had tensed up and with the old lady's hand still resting on me, I could feel her respond with an instinctive pat. *Calm down and get it together Gary. What do you know?* The fact that it was so dark meant that morning was still a way off. The house was still, and since I had awoken, I had heard nothing moving about. Mrs. Abrams appeared to have fallen back to sleep and her breathing was deep and rhythmic. *Time to get out of here.* I was about to jump down to the hardwood floor below and head for the stairs when I remembered what got me into all of this in the first place. Time still seemed to be on my side, so I made my way over to the nightstand to find what I had been looking for. *Where was it? Near the back?* I found the bottle and held it up to my face, turning it, trying to catch any light I could to be able to read the letters. A-n-t-a-c-i-d was written on the bottle. *Antacid? Is that the same thing? I thought the word Jenny had me writing out was longer than that.* Still, it was the closest thing I had found so far, so I decided to take the bottle with me.

I jumped down onto the floor and headed towards the bedroom door. Before entering the hallway, I gave a long listen, just to see if I could detect Mr. Pickles prowling around the house. After a few cautious minutes, I mustered up the courage to head out of the bedroom. *Get out of the house now!* The words were exploding over and over in my head. I almost broke for the stairs when I remembered the other bathroom on the second floor. *Might be my only chance to check.* As I entered the bathroom, I noticed that it looked very similar to the one downstairs, just a little bit bigger. The sink had a mirror over it that protruded out from the wall just like the downstairs bathroom, so that is where I started my search. I jumped up onto the basin and tugged at the mirror as I had before. The door swung open and I saw a plethora of pill bottles placed on the shelves inside. Most of the names were too long for me to read. They all ended in -ithin or -othone. I found a bottle of pills that was about half full and started reading the label. *Erythromycin. Take this antibiotic twice daily . . . This is it! Antibiotic!* I grabbed the bottle with the pills and jumped down from the bathroom sink, leaving the mirrored door open in my haste. I ran to the top of the stairs with both bottles tucked under my arm. Hesitating at the top of the stairs, I listened intently for even the slightest sound before descending. *Nothing.* I made my way down to the first floor, this time not even slowing for the creaks and moans of the old steps and burst into the hallway. Confident that the coast was clear, I headed towards the exit and to the safety of the woodland beyond.

I know I should have kept on going and headed right out of the cat door and into Jenny's waiting arms, but as I passed by the first door to the kitchen, an irresistible smell caught my attention. *What is it? It smells creamy and rich and fatty all at the same time.* A tug of war between my fear and my hunger began. One part of me was still screaming inside my head to get out and not push my luck. Another part of me was rumbling, doing its best to convince me that we had plenty of time, whispering: 'why not check out what that tempting smell is?' I stood in the hall waiting to see which part of me would win out when the thought struck me. *Maybe this is something I could bring to Emma as well, to help her get her strength back; Mission goal number three.* With an altruistic motive in hand, I made the familiar choice to indulge my belly over responding to common sense.

I followed the smell to the kitchen counter next to the sink. The intoxicating aroma grew stronger the closer I got. I leapt up on to the counter to discover a plate with a yellow brick that gleamed at me as if it were made of pure gold. I dipped one finger into the yellow substance and gave it a taste. *Pure fat.* It was like nothing I had ever tasted before. I dipped my finger in again, then my whole hand. Soon licking my hand was not enough and I gorged myself by putting my whole face into the creamy yellow substance. *Divine.* The next thing I knew, half of the brick had disappeared. My belly was full to the point of being a little sick, but it was all worth it. *So rich and creamy.* It was in that blissful moment, that I heard the sound of a cat flap swinging open and closed and what I could have sworn was the cry of a crow, cawing in the distance.

CHAPTER 24

Trapped

THE PEACEFUL FEELING I WAS enjoying with a belly full of butter soon turned to dread as I realized that my time had run out and Mr. Pickles had returned home. Right away he knew something was wrong. Pickles froze in the hallway and I could hear him feverishly sniffing the air trying to figure out what was happening and who was there. *Think Gary, think!* I instantly regretted my detour into the kitchen. *Why is my stomach always getting me into trouble? Ok, options. The basement exit is blocked. The cat door is blocked. The only option is to get upstairs to Mrs. Abrams' bedroom window and claw my way out. Great plan if I were still upstairs, but I would have to jump down, run up the noisy stairs and chew through the screen before Pickles or Mrs. Abrams got to me. I should have chewed through the screen when I was up there just in case I needed it. Another lesson learned. When things are calm, prepare for the problems of the future.*

As I was hearing Mr. Pickles slowly advancing, still sniffing the air as he moved up the steps from the entrance to the sitting area, another option now presented itself to me. *Sink Gary, sink!* Hunker down in the kitchen and hope for the best. I had been all over the house, so there was no telling which scent trail he would follow. If he went down to the basement first, I could sprint for the door. If he followed the trail to the bedrooms upstairs, it might lead him past the kitchen, once again opening a window to escape unseen.

I slunk down into the stainless-steel sink and curled myself into a ball to stay as low as I could so that anyone looking up at the counter would not see me. At least that was the idea. I shivered a bit as I lay there in the cold, metallic sink. I could hear Mr. Pickles moving into the hallway, getting closer and closer. He started uttering some deep guttural sounds, like the cat version of a growl. It was very unnerving. He knew there was an intruder in the house, and now he was getting ready for the hunt.

Downstairs! downstairs! If I continued repeating the thought in my head often enough, maybe it might influence the old tomcat's choices. At first, it seemed like it was working. I heard him turn back from the hallway and descend the first couple of stairs to the basement. He was confused by all the overlapping scent trails. As I hid out in the sink, wondering how much time I should give him and if I should spring from my hiding spot, he turned around and headed back into the main floor living room. Sounding even angrier and more vengeful, he reentered the hallway.

As he passed the first opening to the kitchen without even stopping, a glimmer of hope flickered in my mind. I could hear him padding along in the hallway when he came to a sudden and abrupt stop at the other entrance to the kitchen. Something had caught his attention. *Can he see me? Smell me?* My heart sank as I tried to will myself into becoming one with the sink, holding my breath in case my inhalations were causing my chest to rise, thereby making me visible to Pickles and revealing my location. Now there was nothing but silence, and even without the sound of my breath, I could not hear anything — no steps, no noises. Cats can be so quiet when they want to. I could not tell if he was still standing motionless in the entrance, if he was doing a search of the kitchen, or perhaps even standing right above me. The silence was broken by another low growl. He smelled something but was still in the doorway. *Come on kitty, go check on your lady.* I was really starting to hate that cat.

Mr. Pickles scanned the kitchen for the intruder. The scent was strong but even with his remarkable night vision, he could see nothing. "Pickles! Pickles! Where are you?" Mrs. Abrams' sleepy voice could be heard from the upstairs. "Here kitty, kitty, kitty," she was calling for her beloved pet.

With that, Mr. Pickles turned and bounded up the stairs to check on his owner. My window of opportunity was open, and I was going to take it. I stood up in the sink and jumped on to the counter. I looked over at the half-eaten stick of fat that remained and came to a realization: it was the only evidence that I had left behind of my presence. *How could I have been so stupid?* While feeling regret for thinking with my belly rather than my head, I got a sudden and brilliant idea. There was one more thing I had to do before I left. I reached out with my hands to the soft, undisturbed portion of butter that remained. Curling my fingers, I pressed my hands firmly and deeply into the soft surface. It made a perfect paw print, not unlike a cat's paw print. I kept my fingers curled up and used my buttery hands to make a few more prints on the counter, then on the floor of the kitchen, and finally on the rug in the sitting room. *Take that Mr. Pickles.*

I burst through the cat flap without giving any thought to the signals we had set up and ran to the bushes where Jenny was supposed to be waiting. "What happened? What took so long? I was so worried! Did you see Mr. Pickles? Didn't you hear me crowing?" She was grabbing me by the shoulders and shaking me as she barraged me with questions.

"I think we had better get out of here," I urged, mustering up as much composure as possible for someone who had just narrowly avoided the claws and teeth of what is essentially a puma in a 20 pound package. I showed Jenny the two bottles of medicine I had stolen from the house. Before she could say another word, I grabbed her by the paw, and we started running for the forest.

CHAPTER 25

Trouble at the Williams'

OTIS WILLIAMS LOVED HIS CHICKENS. Every morning, after his first cup of black coffee, he would head outside to let the chickens out of their coop so they could roam about in the back yard. He would then collect a half dozen or so fresh, brown eggs and proudly present them to his wife, hoping that she would then turn them into his breakfast. The task of caring for them was getting more difficult as Otis got older. He used to throw the 50-pound bags of chicken feed over his shoulder and carry them out to the henhouse without even thinking about it. But now he found it difficult to even lift them into the wheelbarrow. Cleaning out the hay and manure happened less and less frequently, much to the chagrin of Felicity Jackson who had the misfortune of being downwind most days.

"Otis!" she would say if she could catch him outside, "those chickens are stinking to high heaven again! If you don't clean up after those chickens, I am going to have to do something about it!" Felicity meant that she would call the city to complain. Otis never did like the sound of her threats. "You know I am trying to take some pictures out here." Her voice would get a little whiny at this point. "Do you know how hard it is to get to kids to not make faces while I am photographing them? Because of the smell emanating from your chicken house, Emily hasn't unwrinkled her nose all morning!" Otis would give the customary apology and get to work cleaning out the coop. The old hay and manure made wonderful compost for the garden. Once turned under and into some soil, the smell would disappear.

It was on one fateful night that Otis' age caught up with him. He and Esther had enjoyed a late dinner that night. Esther had made a wonderful pot roast with potatoes and carrots. A nice bottle of wine had capped off the evening. The forecast had called for rain that afternoon, but the precipitation did not start until the evening. By the time Otis had finished his dinner, the rain was pouring down. He had meant to go out and close up the chickens right after sundown before the storm started. Now looking outside, he thought to himself maybe he would wait an hour or so to see if it would let up or not. Pouring himself another glass of wine, he and Esther sat and watched the television for a while. Soon they both dozed off on the couch, and only woke up enough to get themselves into bed.

By the next morning, the rain had stopped and the sun was shining again. Otis enjoyed his usual cup of black coffee, and after reading through the newspaper he decided it was time to go get some eggs for his breakfast. It did not take long for him to realize something had gone terribly wrong at the henhouse. As he approached, he noticed that there were feathers everywhere, as if someone had cut open a pillow and spewed its contents all over the lawn. He had a sinking feeling in his gut as he remembered he did not make it out the previous night to close the coop door. Looking into the henhouse he could see dead chickens everywhere. Most of them had their heads removed from their bodies. He looked around to see if there were any survivors, but nothing was moving inside on that fateful morning. All twelve chickens had been decapitated.

Otis stared in shock at the devastation of his beloved chickens. He thought at worst a predator would take one or two chickens and make a meal out of them. Never did it cross his mind that they could all be wiped out in one evening should he forget to close the door. As Otis stood there dumbfounded, he was completely unaware that he was being watched.

CHAPTER 26

A Life Saved?

JENNY AND I WENT DIRECTLY from Mrs. Abrams' place to the home of the porcupine family. Jenny went straight in to check on little Emma. Her fever was still running high and you could hear the sad little coughs of a girl who was tired of coughing. "Do you know how much Emma weighs?" Jenny asked.

"About six pounds I think," Gwendolyn answered.

Jenny started to scratch some numbers into the dirt floor with her fingers. "Ok, we got the medicine for Emma. You are going to have to take one of these pills and try to divide it into eight dosages. It might be a little strong, but it should do the trick. Make sure she gets plenty of water." Jenny counted out four of the pills from the container I took from Mrs. Abrams' bathroom. "You will need to give her one dosage of the pills, three times a day until all of the medicine is used up. Even when she is feeling better, she still has to take the medicine. If she stops it could come back even worse. Do you understand?"

Gwendolyn nodded. "Thank you so much, Jenny. I don't know what we would've done without you. To you too Mr. Raccoon, thank you so much!" She leaned in to give me a little kiss on the cheek. I blushed, stammering away about how it was nothing, and that I was happy to help. Jenny assured her that we would be back in a few days to check on

Emma's progress and that if she needed anything to send someone to come get her.

As we were about to exit the den Jenny turned to Gwendolyn and asked, "By the way, is your husband still losing his quills?"

Gwen seemed to be taken aback by this question so out of context. "Why yes, he is. I guess it happens to a lot of men. Porcupine pattern baldness. The most annoying thing is him shedding all over the house." She continued to grumble even after she finished speaking.

"Any chance you could save some quills for me, put them in a box or something? I have a project they would be perfect for." Jenny asked in a sweet and casual way, trying not to give any indication of what she might need a box full of porcupine quills for.

"Sure. Anything for you Jenny," the perplexed porcupine replied, as she watched us leave up the tunnel and into the night.

CHAPTER 27

The Hills Have Eyes

OTIS WAS NOT AWARE OF all the eyes that were watching him at that moment. Beyond his fence, on the hillside that rose from the back of his property, a fox and a chipmunk were staring intently at the scene below. They had concealed themselves behind a rocky outcrop, safe from the view of anyone in the homes below who might by chance look up at the hillside. Quietly, they watched as Otis Williams discovered the carnage in the chicken coop.

There was another pair of eyes that was gazing intently at him as he surveyed the bodies of his beloved poultry. Thomas Jackson had been peering through the fence when Otis had stepped out of his house in search of his breakfast. Thomas was an unusual boy. To say that he was quiet would be an understatement. He rarely spoke, and when he did it was just a few words. Complete sentences were even rarer. At one point when he was almost three years old, Felicity had taken him to the doctor because he still had not spoken his first word. The doctor referred him to a local speech-language specialist, but no obvious medical or developmental reason for his silence was found. He scored extremely high on the intelligence tests, including being able to identify letters and words at an advanced level for his age. Physically there was nothing wrong with him either; it was as if he just chose not to vocalize. "Some children just take longer to start talking," was the doctor's final assessment. With that Felicity was left to stuff her anxiety deep down inside and pretend like everything was normal. Finally, at about age four a few words started to trickle out. Even after it became obvious that he knew how to speak, it just seemed that he preferred not to.

His quietness though transcended his refusal to speak. Even from a young age, he had a way of sliding in right next to someone without their being aware of his presence. More than a few of the Jacksons' family and friends had been startled when — in the middle of a conversation — they realized Thomas had been standing there watching them for some time without any of them realizing.

He was also an unusually observant child. He would always be silently watching and remembering the details of all the events going on around him. One time when he was just five years old his mother had lost the label maker she used to help organize her kitchen. Felicity called out to her husband, "Ethan, have you seen the label maker? I thought I put it here in this kitchen drawer." Frustrated she started pulling open each of the drawers in the kitchen, just to make sure it had not been misplaced by accident.

"Sorry, I haven't seen it, honey," Ethan answered back from the den in the disinterested way that husbands sometimes do. As she closed the last drawer, she turned and jumped at the sight of Thomas standing behind her.

"Oh, I'm sorry sweetie, I didn't hear you come up behind me. Mommy was just looking for her label maker." Thomas stood there silently for what seemed an uncomfortably long period of time, and then without saying a word, he turned and headed into the living room and opened the door on the bottom of the entertainment center. He removed the label maker and brought it to his mother. "Oh, there it is! You clever boy! Where did you find it?" Thomas just pointed in the direction of the living room. "Thank you! By the way, how did you know it was there?" You could hear the gears turning in Felicity's head as she knew she would never have put it there. Thomas just looked at his mother, and then turned and headed to the den to watch television with his Dad. This was not the only incident of its kind. Thomas seemed to have an uncanny knack of knowing where everything was. It was to the point that Ethan and Felicity wondered if he was moving things around and hiding them, just so he could be the one to find them later.

It was this same pair of young eyes that was now watching Otis through the fence, observing intently as Otis shook his head in both disbelief and grief, watching as Otis got his wheelbarrow out and started to clean up the bodies and feathers of his now-dead chickens.

From the vantage point on the hill, Max and Jonathan had a clear view of both the Williams' and Jacksons' back yards. They both noticed the little boy keenly watching from the other yard. "Do you see that boy staring through the fence, Max? Do you think he could have had anything to do with what happened here? It's not normal to be so fascinated by all those dead bodies, is it?" Jonathan was hopeful Max would have some sort of answer.

"Hard to tell with the humans, boys especially. I have heard stories of human boys killing animals for no reason. Not sure the boy just gawking through the fence is evidence enough to convict him of anything though. He docs appear to be unusually intense in his observation of the other human."

Otis, on the other hand, was a little quicker to rush to judgment. He had noticed that the chickens had not been eaten; just the heads had been removed. At that very moment he noticed young Thomas staring at him through the fence. "Hey, you, boy! Do you know anything about what happened to my chickens? Did you see anything?" Otis started walking over to the fence, the body of a dead chicken in hand, waving it in the direction of the Jackson boy. Thomas' silence indicated guilt as much as any confession could have in Otis' eyes. "Answer me, boy! Did you have anything to do with what happened to these animals? I see you looking over here all the time. What did you do?" Thomas just looked up at him with wide eyes and a blank expression on his face.

Otis had almost reached the fence by this time. He was convinced that the boy was involved somehow and that he was hiding something. "So, you did have something to do with this! You miserable little brat! Why I should climb over this fence right now . . ."

It was at this moment Felicity Jackson arrived on the scene. "Why are you yelling at my son? Get away from him!" She pulled Thomas away from the fence and instinctively pushed him behind her.

"Listen, Felicity," Otis said, as he regained his composure and calmed himself down a little. "Last night something or someone got into my chicken coop and killed all of my chickens. I say someone because it doesn't look like any predator I've seen. Animals kill for food and take what they need. This was something different. Whoever it was killed every chicken in the house and just left the bodies behind. Nothing has been eaten at all. I was just asking the boy if he had seen anything last night. I'm sorry, I didn't mean to raise my voice at the child. I'm just upset over this whole thing," he backpedaled a little as the boy's guilt did not seem so conclusive with his mother present.

"Well, I am sorry about your smelly chickens. Thomas was in bed last night and couldn't possibly have seen anything. Don't you talk to my children like that ever again! If you want to ask them something you come and talk to me!" With that, Felicity took her son by the hand and stomped off toward her house. After a few steps, with his mother pulling at his arm, Thomas slowly turned his head and looked back over his shoulder and directly at Otis.

CHAPTER 28

A Question of Trust

MAX AND JONATHAN SPENT THE better part of the afternoon watching the happenings in the back yards of the people that lived below. They witnessed Otis Williams begin his day in the usual way, only to go from confusion to shock and disbelief. They saw the little boy watching the emotional drama of his elderly neighbor with disturbing concentration. They saw the whole exchange between Otis and Felicity Jackson. They were even watching when Otis had to bury the bodies of his chickens in the back corner of his property, only to return to his house sullen and defeated.

Max wanted to take a look at the crime scene himself after the neighborhood quieted down and most everyone had retired for the evening. They hunkered down behind the rocks, content to wait until the evening light had faded and they could begin their investigation. The pair sat quietly, contemplating the events of the past few days. As the sun started to set, basking the forest in a warm, orange light, Jonathan was the one who broke the silence. "Max, can I ask you something?"

The question pulled Max out of his pondering, "Sure Jonathan, what's on your mind?"

Jonathan paused, as if he were summoning the courage to utter his next words. "Have you ever eaten a chipmunk before?"

The question caught Max by surprise, and he turned to look at his little friend. "Why would you ask me that?" Jonathan's eyes did not meet Max's gaze but continued looking out at the homes below.

"I have been thinking about the nature of this case. Since the usual motivations do not appear to be behind the killings, it got me thinking a lot about the imbalance that exists in relationships; from the humans to the animals that exist around them; from the domesticated animals that live with the humans to the forest creatures. Even in our world, we see the power that the predators maintain over their fearful prey. That got me thinking about you and me. I think of you as a trusted friend, but I cannot deny that it is your nature is to be the predator and I, your prey. So that got me wondering, have you ever eaten a chipmunk?"

Max returned to looking at the homes and the valley below. Only a small portion of the sinking sun was still visible above the horizon and now the trees and the homes cast long shadows over the tranquil neighborhood. The whole area was bathed in strips of light and darkness. Max thought for a while before he answered his friend. "I suppose I might have eaten a chipmunk or two in my lifetime; none recently, if that makes you feel any better." Normally that is where Max would have hoped for a laugh to lighten the moment. Sensing the mood, he kept his tone and cadence deliberate and serious. "It is true that all creatures have needs and desires that they strive to fulfill. They use whatever power or advantage they have to satisfy those wants. In the case of the humans, they use their intelligence and tools to try and control the animals in the forest. The domestic animals use their social power to gain leverage over the humans. Their cohabitation with their human allies gives them the advantages of food, shelter, and security. Predators like myself use our size and strength to take what we need from those less powerful. That seems to be the nature of the world around us."

"It is more than that don't you think?" Jonathan replied. "So many times, the exercise of that power goes beyond the basic needs of survival and self-preservation, as if the exercise of that authority over others in and of itself becomes a driving force. Like what we see below us in the Williams' back yard. Is all that destruction just because someone could? How do we explain such cruelty in the absence of any apparent necessity? Is this where our world is heading, out of balance, with everyone focused solely on their own advantage and interest? If so, is it only a matter of time before our very nature destroys all of our relationships and the world around us?" This time Jonathan looked directly at Max, with eyes that held both fear and hope.

Max looked at his little friend and for the first time saw the world through his eyes. He had never even considered that he might have reason to be afraid of him. Being the one in a position of power, he had just assumed that Jonathan felt the same bond of friendship that he did. He wondered if in times past he had used his advantages over Jonathan in order to circumvent his preferences or to dismiss his opinions on matters. Had he ever been afraid to disagree? Was theirs truly an equal and open partnership, or was the balance tipped too much in his favor? Max turned away from his friend and gazed out over the darkening valley as he gathered his thoughts.

"I think the answer to your question requires looking beyond our apparent nature. Are we just animals looking to satisfy our physical needs and impulses, working together only when it is to our advantage, and subsequently discarding those very partnerships when the sacrifices outweigh the benefits? Many examples can be found of this. I believe that we can decide to be something more. Take a look at those leaves on the ground. Do you notice how they are at the mercy of the wind, being blown about in every direction, with no control over their destination? That does not have to be who we are, simply blown about by our needs and desires. In contrast, do you see the oak tree in the distance? Do you know that tree?

It has to be one of the largest around here." Jonathan gave a nod as he looked out at the massive tree that rose behind the houses of Eleanor Place.

"That tree is not simply at the mercy of the wind for its direction in life. When the winds come, it may bend or sway, but it stays in its place, true to what it is. I believe we can be like that. We can choose to be firm in who we are; to decide to be the kind of person we know we should be, even if at times it is inconvenient or leaves us at a disadvantage." Max crouched down to be at the same level as his little friend. "Whatever you might wonder about my nature, I choose to be something more. I choose to be your friend. I know that there is nothing I could need or want, nothing that could happen in my life that would ever change that." Jonathan looked into the caring eyes of the wise, old fox and felt some comfort. With all the terrible things that had happened recently, at least there was one thing he knew he could count on.

The loyal pair was suddenly distracted by a commotion of activity going on down on the street below. The humans were coming out of their houses and heading toward the center of the cul-de-sac. They could hear the muffled sounds of many voices all talking at once. Otis Williams was waving at his neighbors as they streamed out of their homes, calling them all together. As curious as Max and Jonathan were as to what the humans were up to, they both realized that there would never be a better time to investigate the crime scene, so they started their descent of the hillside.

CHAPTER 29

Otis Calls a Meeting

OTIS WILLIAMS HAD NOT BEEN content to just lay about his house after the death of his chickens. The whole situation did not sit right with him, not to mention the disconcerting little boy next door. He kept playing the events over and over in his mind. He felt as if he had to do something. "Why don't you talk to some of the neighbors dear," Esther Williams was trying to think of what she could do to help comfort her husband. "Maybe someone saw something that can help you figure out what happened." At first, in his agitated state, Otis dismissed the idea. But the more he thought about it, the more he realized it might be the only way to figure anything out.

Late that morning, he decided to make up a flyer and left a copy at every house on the street. On bright red paper with black lettering he wrote:

Seeking information on a terrible crime.
One dozen lives have been lost.
Will you be next?
Please meet in the middle of the cul-de-sac after sundown.
Cordially,
Your neighbor, Otis Williams

Esther tried to convince him that it was a little too over the top, but Otis insisted that he needed to get their attention or else no one would show up. Sure enough, at sundown people came out of their houses, flyer in hand, to try and figure out what on earth was going on.

"Otis, what is the meaning of this?" Ethan Jackson and his family were the first to arrive. "Is this about your chickens? And why were you yelling at my boy this afternoon? I have heard of nothing else from Felicity from the moment I got home tonight!" He was hoping to continue his rant when John and Elizabeth Sampson, as well as the Asters, came out to the center of the cul-de-sac. Mrs. Abrams was the last one to arrive, but they could see her coming in the distance.

"Otis, what is the meaning of this flyer you left in our door? What in the world is going on?" Claude Aster could sound quite intimidating when he wanted to.

"Hold on everyone, I will explain everything. Let's just wait for Mrs. Abrams." The group watched as the old woman slowly made her way to meet them. "Good evening Abigail," Otis called out, waving for her to join them. Mrs. Abrams gave a nod to everyone and joined the group.

"Thank you all for coming out tonight," Otis began. "Let me tell you what happened this morning and why I called this meeting." Otis laid out the events of the day, how he had found all of his chickens dead, how the heads had been removed and the bodies had just been left there and that in the course of a single night, not one of them had been left alive. He tried to make the details as grisly and ghastly as he could, and at the same time see if he could learn anything from the reactions of his neighbors as he laid out the story.

"The reason why I asked you here tonight is twofold. First, I wanted to know if any of you maybe saw something last night, perhaps an animal prowling around, or maybe a strange car in the area; any information that might help me figure out who did this. Secondly, I wanted to warn you all. If it happened to me, it could happen to you. I think you all need to be on guard and make sure that your pets are safe until we get to the bottom of this." Most everyone was staring at the ground when Otis finished speaking.

John Sampson was the first to break the silence. "That is terrible Otis, I am so sorry this happened to you." The others nodded in agreement. "But why would you ask about a car? Do you think it could be a person who did this? Surely it must have been a coyote or some other animal that did it, right?" John was looking at the others for support.

"I don't know who or what did this," Otis said. "All I know is that hungry animals usually take what they can eat. As far as I can tell, all the bodies were left to rot. It just don't make a lick of sense." Claude Aster noticed that Otis kept glancing over at Felicity and Thomas as he spoke. "Did anyone see anything suspicious?" There was a note of desperation in Otis' voice.

"I'm sorry Otis," Claude Aster replied. "With the rain and thunder last night we didn't see anything. I have to admit, human or animal, if you wanted to hide your tracks and go unnoticed, last night would have been the perfect night. Even if a car had driven up, I'm not sure we would have heard it."

All the other neighbors made similar statements about the weather. No one had seen or heard anything unusual the previous night. That is when Elizabeth Sampson spoke up. "I didn't see anything last night either, but now that you mention it, I have been finding more dead animals in the yard than usual, squirrels and birds, that kind of thing. Do you think it could mean anything?"

One by one the neighbors shared stories that by themselves could easily be overlooked, but upon hearing them all together, an uneasy feeling settled over the group.

"My friend Sue, who lives down on Elm Street, she told me that her cat has been missing for over three weeks, and she heard that her neighbor was looking for their Yorkie."

Julia Aster added to the conversation, "I wonder how many other pets in the area have gone missing." With that, the group got quiet again as they all started to process this new information.

"Well, there you have it. So now we are left with the question of who or what is doing this and what can we do about it. How do we protect our pets and other animals?" Otis asked.

"We could set some traps," Mrs. Aster offered. "My husband has a bunch of live animal traps he used to use. Some of them are big enough for a coyote or anything else that might be prowling around in these woods. I would be happy to let you use them, Otis. They are in the shed out back," she said as she gestured toward her back yard. "Then we shall see who it was that got into your chickens." The old lady's voice had a note of finality, and with no other suggestions proffered, everyone agreed to the plan and said goodnight. Claude Aster offered to give Otis a hand setting up the traps around the neighborhood the following day. They were to meet for lunch at Otis' place and draw up a map for the placement of the traps. With everyone satisfied, they headed back to their homes for the remainder of the evening.

CHAPTER 30

Max calls a Meeting

WITH THE HUMANS ALL IN one location, Max and Jonathan knew they had the perfect window of opportunity to move about in the back yards of both the Jacksons and the Williams without fear of being noticed. After looking around, they concluded that this crime appeared to be consistent with the other killings they had investigated in its absence of an apparent motive. Max had hoped for some physical evidence, something definitive that would identify which world the killer belonged to — human or animal. Between the rain and the fact that Otis has cleaned everything up, there was not much left to go on. The only piece of evidence he found at all was an unusual, red smudge on the frame of the door. It looked similar to a human handprint, only smaller. It was hard to tell how long it had been there.

Max had sent Jonathan to investigate the Jackson's property, and they were to meet back at the rocky outcrop when they had both finished their investigations. "Well, that was a bust. Maybe if we had gotten a look this morning, we would have found more clues to crack this case open. As it stands, I found nothing to indicate who is behind all of this. Any clue that might have existed is gone now, washed away by the rain." Max could hear in Jonathan's voice that he was getting discouraged.

"That is my assessment as well. All the physical evidence has been degraded to the point that conclusions cannot be drawn. While many of the things we saw fit multiple theories, we are no closer to identifying our killer. Still, we did learn one especially important fact. The humans that gathered together tonight are no doubt preparing a response to whatever they think happened here. It is just a matter of time before they blame us, those who live in the forest, for the death of their fowl. I think we should follow their lead and call a meeting of our own.

Max and Jonathan headed back into the forest. Along the way, they urged anyone they encountered to be present at a meeting of all the animals in the valley the following morning. They also were to spread the word to as many as possible. Max had tasked some of the blue jays and ravens with flying over the forest in the early hours of the morning, to sound the call for all to gather. They were to meet just after sunrise at Elephant Rock.

As the first few glimmers of the morning light appeared over the horizon, the birds took to the sky and sounded the alarm. Soon everyone in the forest was awake and heading to the clearing. By the time the sun had risen the meadow was full of all kinds of animals, great and small. Max waited until the light streamed through the trees into the meadow, striking the great rock in such a way that it seemed to glow.

The time had come for Max to speak. He climbed up on to the large boulder and looked out upon the gathering of animals below. Upon raising his arm, the whole congregation fell silent and turned their attention upon him. "Ladies and gentlemen, birds and beasts, I have called you all here today to warn you of a very grave threat. A predator has been prowling this forest for the past several weeks and we have lost some good animals. As you know, Jonathan and I have been investigating these killings, trying to find out who is responsible. While we do not yet know who it was that perpetrated these crimes, we do know a few things. This has not been the work of a new alpha predator, or that of any of the other usual animals that come here to hunt. No, this has been the work of something vastly different. There is no known reason for the crimes; no gnawing hunger that needs a meal. This killer takes lives for reasons that are his own and seems to find no satiation from the kill. That makes him the most dangerous predator of all. Even the humans' animals have been attacked without fear. We have recently witnessed the work of this killer in the death and destruction of the Williams' chickens. Not one of them was left alive."

The noise of concerned voices started to rise among the congregated animals. "Not *one* left alive? How could that be?"

"Even the *humans* could not keep them safe?"

"Who could do a thing like this?" The concern was quickly turning into fear.

Max continued to speak. "We do not know if this predator is human or animal; a stranger to these parts, or someone familiar to us all." With that statement, the sound of murmured conversations from the crowd began to rise again. "But we do know one thing," Max raised his voice as loud as he could without yelling. The crowd quieted down as they again turned their attention back to Max. "We do know one thing," Max repeated this time in a softer voice. "The humans have put the blame squarely on us and are preparing their response as we speak. They are declaring war on the animals of the forest and we need to prepare for our defense."

Again, Max lost control of the crowd as the fervor of hundreds of voices rose. As the murmuring masses coalesced their fears into one voice, Robert Badger approached the rock and called out from the crowd, "How are we supposed to protect ourselves from the humans? They are too powerful for us. They have poisons and guns and who knows how many other ways to kill us. We can't possibly defeat them! The minute we strike back they will level this forest and destroy everything!" From the response of the crowd, it was clear that most were feeling the same way.

"It is true that we cannot defeat the humans in a direct confrontation. What we can defeat is their animosity toward us. We are many, and if we are united, we are unstoppable. Our strength must lie in unity. If we work together, we can confront and neutralize any danger." A hopeful feeling started to rise in those gathered in the clearing. "Information is the most powerful tool we have at our disposal. We must begin immediate surveillance of the humans. We must figure out how they plan to move against us. Only then will we be able to defend ourselves." Max's voice included a call to action that suddenly caused the crowd to go quiet, as the instinct of most animals is to stay as far away from humans as possible. The thought of being close enough to the humans to observe them sent a wave of primal fear through the entire congregation. The hush that ensued was almost deafening. Paralyzed by fear, the crowd stood momentarily motionless.

The silence was broken by movement at the back of the crowd. "Excuse me, pardon me, can we get through?" The soft feminine voice was the only sound to be heard other than the shuffling of feet and paws as the other animals moved out of the way. Soon the attention of the entire gathering was turning to see who was behind the disturbance. As Jenny and Gary tried to make their way through the throng to the center, to the speaker standing atop Elephant Rock, a strange thing happened. The stunned crowd parted like the Red Sea, opening a pathway through the multitude, leading directly to the main stage. All watched in silence as a rabbit and a raccoon walked the gauntlet to arrive at the base of the rock. Max looked down at the unlikely pair as they approached.

With the whole crowd intently watching, Max inquired: "And what can you two do to help protect the forest?"

Jenny looked up at the regal fox, bathed in the rays of the morning sun. "We can surveil the humans. We can discover their plans and protect all of those gathered here today. We can get close enough to the humans to learn everything we need to be safe." The crowd again began to murmur and scoff at the idea that a raccoon and rabbit could even come close to accomplishing such a thing.

"Are you fools?" said Robert Badger, who was still standing at the base of the rock. "Raccoons are public enemy number one to the humans! 'Trash bandits' they call you, and rabbits? Thieves of the garden! You would both be shot as soon as the humans saw you! Max, you can't possibly think this preposterous pair could be of any use?"

Max raised his paw to silence the blustering badger. "Is this possible? Are you able to get close enough to the humans to learn of their plans?" Max's sincere inquiry moved Jenny to speak.

"We can. Please let us do this for our people. We can get the information you seek and help to save all of us gathered here today." Jenny's claim once again provoked the voice of dissent from a considerable number in the crowd.

After contemplating the rabbit's claim for a few moments, Max raised his hands to the crowd once again. The voices died down to the point that it was quiet enough for Max to speak. "Many of you doubt the brash claims of this bold bunny. Do any of you offer an alternative? Do any of you volunteer to go into the human world and gather the information we need?" There was an overwhelming silence in the meadow in response to Max's question. "Seeing as none of you are willing or able to do so, we have no choice but to put our fate into the paws of these courageous companions." All eyes again turned to the couple at the base of the rock. "Go! And report back to me in no more than two or three days. Time is of the essence. For the rest of you: avoid the human world at all costs. It may mean your life! We will send word when we know more." With that Max motioned to the gathering to disperse, and the animals slowly left the meadow and returned to their homes.

CHAPTER 31

How is Baby Emma?

JENNY AND I WERE AMONG the last to leave the clearing that morning. After the crowd had dispersed, we talked to Max and Jonathan at length about the events that they had been investigating and their possible meaning. They shared with us details of what they had witnessed while watching the Williams' place, the interaction with the Jackson boy, the gathering of the humans in the cul-de-sac, and what they had discovered investigating Otis Williams' chicken coop. There was one clue that they had uncovered at the crime scene that they had not yet shared with anyone else: the single, red handprint that had been left on the chicken coop door frame. Max suspected that it had been made by the killer, but due to his suspicions that it had been made by a human child, they kept the information to themselves so as to not cause a panic. It was too distorted by the night's rain to make a positive identification, but from the size of the palm area and fingers, it was too small to be that of an adult human. To Max and Jonathan, this made the Jackson boy the prime suspect.

Max had made multiple inquiries as to how we would conduct our surveillance and how we could get close enough to the humans to find out what they were up to. I was ready to tell them everything; about how we had entered the homes of several of the humans already and how we had created our disguises of the humans' pets to gain access to their world, but Jenny held me back. "We have our ways," she said politely, "But for the sake of security we feel it is best not to divulge any of the details at this time." I was not sure why she took this approach, but I trusted her and followed her lead. We said our goodbyes to the detective duo and promised to return as soon as possible with a full report.

As we left the meadow, I asked Jenny why she felt we should not reveal to Max our newfound abilities. To be honest, the temptation to boast about our exploits was difficult to control. I wanted everyone to know about what we could do and what we had accomplished. "Here is the thing about a secret identity," Jenny said, "it must remain a secret. As soon as you tell someone — even if it is someone you think you trust — you lose control of the secret. Everyone has someone that they are closer to than they are to you. We might tell Max, but then he will share it with Jonathan. Jonathan, in turn, will have someone close to him that he values more than he does us, and he will share it with that person. The cycle will repeat until soon our secret is not very secret anymore, just something people know they are not supposed to talk about. Soon everyone will be looking to see if they can spot you, find the flaws in your disguises and suddenly we will have lost the ability to impersonate anyone. Once a magician reveals how a trick is done, you are no longer captured by the illusion; your only focus becomes trying to see if you can catch its mechanics as it unfolds. Our impressions are good, but they succeed on the basis that no one even considers the possibility that what they are looking at could be anything different from what they are conditioned to expect. The only way to keep a real secret is to not tell anyone. The only way to keep doing what we have been doing is for no one to even imagine that it can be done. So, you and I are the only ones who can know — no matter what. Do you understand?" I nodded in agreement, but I was not sure I fully understood. I did trust Jenny completely, so I would try my best to keep the impulse to boast in check and not reveal our secret to anyone.

"I want to see how Emma is doing. It has been close to a week now and we are not far from her home. Can we go and see her?" I could never say no to Jenny and was curious myself as to how things with the little porcupine were proceeding, so we headed off to check in on our friends.

When we arrived at the porcupine burrow Jenny once again called out at the entrance, "Hello? Is anyone home? Gwendolyn, are you there?" We waited a few minutes before we heard a voice call out.

"Is that you Jenny? Come in! Come in! We're home. You must come in!" We were surprised by the enthusiastic greeting and hoped it meant good news. Scampering down the entrance and into the open living quarters, we were greeted by the smiling face of Gwendolyn. "Oh, Jenny it is so wonderful to see you!" Gwendolyn threw her arms around Jenny who very carefully tried to return the hug. "You must come and see Emma. I can't thank you enough for what you did for her. I think you saved her life." With that, she led us down the passageway and into Emma's room. When we entered, we saw a healthy, rambunctious child playing with her siblings. Except for the occasional cough, she was as healthy as a horse.

"Aunty Jenny!" Emma cried out when she caught sight of her. She ran and gave Jenny a giant hug.

"My Emma, you look like you are feeling better!" Jenny laughed as she saw before her the vibrant child she had always known.

"Yep feeling all better!" As quickly as she came, Emma ran off and returned to playing with her brothers and sisters.

"See, you saved her life, Jenny. Without that medicine you brought her, I don't know if she would still be alive today. I cannot thank you enough for what you did." Gwen reached out her arm and in a grateful gesture touched Jenny's paw. The unrelenting compliments finally got to Jenny, and for the first time since I had known her, she seemed to be at a loss for words.

"Really it was a joint effort," she blushed a bit as she talked. "It was Gary who did most of the work. We are just happy she is doing so well and is healthy again. We better be on our way. Gary and I have some important work that we need to get back to. I am so happy that Emma is doing so well!"

"Well, thanks then to both of you!" Gwen gave us both big hugs and as we said our goodbyes and started to leave, she blurted out, "Oh wait! I also have what you were asking for. Can you hold on for just a moment?" With that, the plucky porcupine scurried to another corridor of their home. She emerged a few minutes later with a large box. "Here are all the quills I was able to collect for you. Most are from my husband but anything I found lying around I put in the box. We even had some family over during the week, so I was able to add in some of the quills they left behind. I hope it is enough for what you needed," she said as she handed the box to Jenny.

Looking inside the box at its prickly contents Jenny exclaimed, "My goodness, there are enough quills in here to make a whole family of porcupines! Thank you so much, Gwen!"

"It was the least I could do after all you did for my Emma." She gave us both, yet another hug and we headed back to Jenny's place to plan out our surveillance of the humans.

CHAPTER 32

Surveillance

BACK AT JENNY'S PLACE, I started sketching on the whiteboard a new map of the humans' homes and yards, as best as I could remember them. While I drew an overview of the street, adding the houses that circled the cul-de-sac, Jenny sat quietly working with the newly acquired quills. She was painstakingly attaching them to a bodysuit made from a stretchable material. It was a medium grey color and when I put it on it covered me almost entirely, from my legs to the top of my head. Longer quills went on the top and back; shorter quills went along the sides and down the outsides of the legs. The work was difficult, and from time to time she would let out a little yelp when she jabbed herself with a sharp quill tip.

As I progressed in my map drawing, I was able to add a lot more detail than the first map Jenny had put together. It surprised me a little how much information we had gathered in just a short period of time. I was able to add a complete drawing of Mrs. Abrams' place, including details inside the fenced garden, multiple entrances that we were previously unaware of, along with other information about the house's interior. The same went for the Asters' place. I wrote a few sentences about the movement and habits of both the animals and the humans, as well as the time of day that they tended to be active or absent.

Max and Jonathan had provided me with some additional information they had collected on the humans' homes from the day they spent observing them from the hill. That, added to my own observations, allowed me to add details as to the distance from the fences to the houses, rough locations of the living and sleeping quarters, as well as profiles on the individuals that lived inside the homes. Max had mentioned the boy, but to me, Felicity Jackson was the scary one. A skunk friend of mine had warned me after a run-in he had with her that she was unpredictable and out of sync with the natural world around her.

On my map, I put a large red asterisk on the Williams' home because, as Max had explained, he was the human that appeared to be taking the lead in the attack against us. I also added the location of the rocky outcrop on the hill that could serve as an observatory of all the homes on the west side of the street.

On the east side, I already had detailed information on the Asters. Access points in and out of the yard and home were tested and ready to use if necessary. I did not know as much about the Sampsons' place. The back yard was not that far from my childhood home and when we were young, on occasion we would approach the home in search of a meal. The fencing was chain link, easy enough to climb over at any point along the back that bordered the ravine. There was a children's play area and even a couple of ways into the yard across on a tree branch that overhung the fence. All this information, I plotted on the map. I had never seen the interior of the house, but it seemed from the outside that the living quarters were on the main floor and the sleeping areas were upstairs. There was one more detail that we had learned about the Sampsons' place: they had a black cat living in the home.

As I stared at my map, with every last detail I could possibly remember plotted on it, I noticed one thing missing: information as to which disguise could get me into each place without being noticed. The Abrams' place was easy; I drew a picture of myself as Mr. Pickles. It was the same with the Asters'; I drew myself as one of the terriers. I knew I could imitate the black cat of the Sampsons without much difficulty, but it would require a total dye job and that would mean we would have to leave it until last. It would take too long to wash the dye out, and that would rule out the option of transforming into a greyish cat or dog. The Jacksons and the Williams presented a different problem. They had no pets that I could impersonate. Jenny was working on an idea for a chicken suit at one point, but there was no way that I could get my head small enough for that to be even remotely believable. Everyone would immediately spot a freakish Franken-chicken anyway, so we abandoned the idea. Not that there were any chickens left to impersonate anyway.

I had been staring at the map for a while when I looked over at Jenny. She had finished with her sewing, so I asked her to come and see what she thought of my work. She took a long look and said, "You have been able to add a lot more detail. I like the notes on the interior of the homes and the marked entrance and exit points. That could be useful, also the details in the yards. Any one of those items might end up being a hiding place or a waiting area. For example, this area of the Abrams' property, is that some kind of a tractor?"

I nodded, "Yes, it is rusted and abandoned. I am guessing it has been there for many, many years. There are also some old tires and parts of other farming equipment lying on the ground in that area. The grass has grown up around them, but they are there. I tried to be thorough. I showed her the part where I was having trouble and circled the two homes on the west side of the street. "Neither of them has any pets that we can impersonate. Do you have any idea how we might be able to take a look around?" I thought that maybe Jenny would see something I missed.

"Well, Mr. Pickles probably wanders in and out of those yards. You could be him and hope that they like the neighbor's cat." That sounded a little too risky to me. Maybe it would work at the Williams', but I doubted the

Jacksons would be very accommodating. "The other idea would be that instead of trying to blend in and go unnoticed, maybe you could take the opposite approach." I looked at Jenny with a puzzled expression and wondered what on earth she was talking about. "There are two animals in the forest that can travel among the humans without fear. Two animals even they leave alone and dare not interfere with. Instead of trying to blend in, maybe you should let yourself be noticed."

Let myself be noticed? Is she crazy? That sounds like a plan where I'll disappear and never be seen again. Jenny could tell by the stunned look on my face that she needed to offer up some more details.

"Think about it. What are two animals in the area that even the humans won't mess with?" My silence prompted her to answer the question herself. "There is the skunk, whose smell the humans fear so much that they won't even approach the animal. Or there is the porcupine, whose quills are dangerous to anyone who might get near. We now have the ability for you to become either!" She hopped over and grabbed the garment she had been working on. "Behold. The porcupine approximator!" The fabric was indeed completely covered in porcupine quills. It looked so realistic, that if someone saw it lying on the floor, they would think a porcupine just curled up and was taking a nap. Staring at the suit of needles, I started to appreciate the genius of her plan. If by chance I was seen, who would dare approach me while I'm armed to the max with protruding spikes? Even the other animals would be cautious in confronting me, let alone getting close enough to discern the flaws in my disguise. In fact, in this one outfit, I would be able to move freely around the neighborhood. As long as I did not linger too long in one place, the outfit would allow me to get into the pet-free yards and gather what information I could.

"It's mid-afternoon now," Jenny said with a wry smile. "Why don't you slip into something uncomfortable and we go have a look-see at what the humans have been up to? You will need to put your mask on first to hide the black around your eyes again." She handed me the grey mask and I tied it around my head to hide my nefarious markings.

Jenny was not kidding when she joked about the outfit. It was almost impossible to get into without impaling myself on the quills. *How do these critters manage? Or even reproduce for that matter?* After a few failed attempts and a few barbs in my backside, we managed to get me suited up. Once I had squeezed into the stretchy fabric, the sharp objects pointing out of me in all directions were a bit more manageable. Walking was a little difficult to get the hang of as I had to try and avoid poking myself with the short quills sticking out from my legs. Jenny called my awkward shuffling 'perfectly porcupiney', so I just went with it. The elastic material came up around my ears and forehead, effectively flattening my ears against my head and hiding them from view. The quills were all around my face like I was some kind of a prickly sunflower, and it felt a little disconcerting to keep seeing something in my peripheral vision. Looking at myself in the mirror I felt that my fake nose did not sit quite right, but Jenny said it was good enough. "No one will be looking at your nose. All they will see are the spikes covering your body." Jenny had a way of discerning realistic perceptions and filtering out irrational fears. We took some time practicing the impression. The walk came easily. It was sort of a sideways shuffle that the suit lent itself to. The sounds were a little more difficult to emulate. If you have ever wondered what a porcupine sounds like, imagine a baby girl with a raspy voice excitedly trying to tell you something. When I had put together the best adlib porcupine impression I could, Jenny I and headed out to the rocky outcrop on the hill behind the Williams' place.

We arrived late in the afternoon to see Claude Aster and Otis Williams working away in Otis' back yard. They had stacks of large metal boxes set out on the picnic table. A large bowl could be seen on the table and Otis was placing an item from the bowl into each one of the boxes. Even from up on the hill my nose caught the smell of something delicious. It was definitely meat of some kind and it reminded me that it had been a while since I had eaten.

We continued to watch as they placed some of the meat into each of the metal boxes. When they were finished, they each took a metal box in hand and walked to the back of the property. Otis placed one in the chicken coop at the top of the ramp and Mr. Aster placed another along the fence in the back corner of the property. We watched over the next few hours as they would get a box, put a piece of meat inside, and then place it somewhere in the neighborhood. They come back over and over again until there were no more boxes left.

Jenny took note of the location of each box as we watched them get placed. For the yards we could not see, she just made a note of how many boxes had headed in that direction. By sundown, we had counted over fourteen boxes that were placed around the area; most in the yards of the humans, but some of them were even placed on the edge of the forest, concealed, but in a location certain to be discovered. Jenny and I concluded that nothing good could come from the boxes and that they must be part of the humans' plans against the forest creatures. We had to raise the alarm about this new danger. Altering our plans, she headed back to the forest to warn the other animals. I, on the other hand, would continue alone in the surveillance and investigation of the humans — starting with the Jacksons.

CHAPTER 33

Operation - The Jacksons

I HAD TO ADMIT THE Jacksons' place was quite amazing. The entire yard looked like it was about to be featured in a magazine spread. A large open area of perfectly manicured grass was rimmed by immaculate gardens. The flower beds were so neatly edged and mulched they could have been in a botanical garden. A patio area next to the house had a large, rectangular, teak table with seating for eight people. White cushions were tied to the matching teak chairs with a bright, blue accent throw pillow placed on each one. Two large, comfortable sectional couches made up a sitting area around a circular, stone fireplace to the right of the dining table. The yard was so beautiful and undisturbed I wondered if anyone was ever allowed to come outside and enjoy it.

The gardens that bordered the fence were designed so that large shrubs and trees hid the fence boards and provided height to the garden. If you were sitting at the table, it would appear that the shrubbery just blended into the base of the hill and your eyes would see nothing but a wall of greenery. This gave me ample coverage to work my way along the entire length of the yard, staying as close to the fence and as out of sight as possible. I was not sure exactly what I was looking for but felt that I would know it when I saw it. Like Jenny always said, 'It is not about knowing what you are doing, it is about putting yourself in a place where good things can happen'. The goals were clear: look for any information that could help to protect us from the humans and keep an eye open for clues as to who might be behind the killings. A spotlight of suspicion had been shone upon the boy. Now it was my job to see if I could find any evidence to justify the suspicion.

The back fence ran past the far corner of the house and ended at a small, triangular area on the north side of the home, out of sight of the table and seating area. This is where the equipment shed was located and the garbage was kept. Even from a distance, I caught a whiff of gasoline and trash. It seemed to be the most promising area to search for clues, as the rest of the yard seemed to be too sanitized for something incriminating to have been just left lying around. To explore it, I would have to cut across the open grass and expose myself to anyone who might happen to be looking out a window or entering the yard until I rounded the corner of the house to safety. It was a little bit risky, but I decided it would be worth it. Scanning the area, as well as the doors and windows of the home for any signs of life, I took my chance and made a break for the shed. Due to the exertion required to maneuver myself across the grass without any of the quills poking me in my tender areas, my speed was comically slow. Most of the energy of my movement had me swaying from side to side rather than being expressed as forward velocity. To any observer, the sight of a waddling pin cushion strenuously exerting itself would be amusing. But from my perspective, I was a master of disguise just hitting top speed and my adrenaline was pumping.

When I arrived at the shed, I felt confident that no one had seen me. I cautiously checked my surroundings before I leaned up against the shed to catch my breath. *Not much for escape routes.* The fence was solid, with a board on board design, so through it or under it were not options. It was made of wood, so normally I would just sink my claws in and climb over easily. But with the porcupine outfit, it would be a daunting task, not a reliable exit plan. I had a vision of myself stuck halfway up, quills embedded into the wood, my hind feet dangling in the air unable to move.

There was a little gap between the fence and the shed that I could squeeze into and hope to go unnoticed, but if I were discovered it would become an inescapable trap. Second thoughts as to the saneness of my plan were starting to creep into my head, but I shook them off and got to work exploring, deciding it was best to stop wasting time thinking about what could go wrong and just move on to getting the job done as quickly as possible.

The shed doors were chained and locked, but I was able to pry them apart just enough to get a good look inside. There was nothing out of the ordinary, so I moved on to the trash. The cans were inside a small, wooden structure with a lid that came down on top. Fortunately, it was not locked in any way. Standing on a concrete block that was beside the structure, I was able to lift the cover up to get a look inside. Holding the top of the wooden structure with one hand, I was able to reach in and grab the lid of one of the metal garbage cans. It had not been snapped into place, so I easily removed it and used the lid to prop the top open so that I could climb up and take a good look around. I searched the trash thoroughly, ripping open plastic bags and digging into their contents. I found everything from old shoes to banana peels, but nothing that could constitute a threat to the animals in the woods. No evidence could be found of poisons or anything else that might be used in an attack or that could be related to the killings. I guess I was not sure what I was expecting — a pair of children's gloves soaked in the blood of a dozen chickens would have been nice — but I came up empty-handed. Not that I wasn't thorough, I even licked out some of the empty ice cream containers I had found to make sure nothing else had been stored inside them.

I was being particularly painstaking in my search of the bottom of a tub of rocky road, when the sound of a door sliding open caused my heart to skip a beat. I could hear the voices of the humans as they were entering the yard. Frozen in terror, my head completely inside a discarded ice cream pail, I dared not make a sound. After a minute I heard

Felicity Jackson's voice, "Now Thomas you stay outside and play for a while. Mommy has to do some editing of her photos. Whatever you do, do not make a mess back here. Now go and play!" With that, the door slid closed and I could hear Thomas Jackson shuffling around in the back yard.

I thought for sure someone would come around the corner and find me in my precarious pose, but as the minutes passed, I realized just standing there not moving would be of little help no matter what happened next. Regaining my courage, I decided that I needed an escape plan. Creeping down from the garbage bins as quietly as possible, I made my way over to the side of the house where I knew I could not be seen from the back yard. The boy had been silent now for a while and not knowing his location was adding to my anxiety. I felt that the only chance I had to escape was to locate the boy, keep an eye on him until he was distracted or busy, and then dash back in behind the bushes. From the relative safety of the bushes, I could silently make my way to the broken fence board in the far corner that I had used to get into the yard in the first place, while remaining unseen for all but a few moments.

I did contemplate shedding my disguise and just going over the wooden fence where I was. Remembering that it took two of us to get me into the porcupine suit in the first place, and the fact that I would end up exposed on the street to whatever new dangers that might be lurking on the other side, I decided against that plan and set my mind to retracing my steps. The fact that Jenny would kill me if I lost my new disguise so soon after she had made it was another motivating factor. As quietly as I could, I prepared myself to look around the corner. Holding my breath, I closed my eyes and listened intently for any danger before I took a glance.

To my surprise, what I heard was the sound of little Thomas giggling. It was faint, but it was unmistakably laughter. He was also talking to someone in soft quiet tones. I wondered if another person had entered the yard unbeknownst to me, maybe another child. I tried to distinguish any other voices. After listening carefully for a while, I determined three things: 1) Thomas was the only one talking, in fact he had not stopped talking the entire time, 2) he was not alone, and 3) he sounded very happy. The last one caught me a bit off guard because it did not seem to fit with my image of him as a crazed, chicken-slaying child.

In order to learn what I was facing, the only thing left for me to do was to poke my head around the corner of the house and hope I would not be noticed. With no clues to go on other than Thomas' voice, I waited until the moment felt right, and then stuck my head out for a little look. *Did I really just see that?* I had gone so quickly that I needed to close my eyes tightly to try and confirm the image that was still dancing on my rods and cones before it faded. Thomas was indeed not alone. He was sitting in the middle of the grassy area, playing with my old friend — Mr. Pickles.

CHAPTER 34

Jenny Finds a Box

JENNY HAD LEFT THE SAFETY of the rocky outcrop to head back to the forest and tell Max about the metal boxes we had seen the humans working on. She was following the old, barbed wire fence at the back of the Williams' property to get to Mrs. Abrams' place, and then to the forest beyond. When she had traveled the length of the fence, she reached the point where it turned east along the border that separated the Williams' and the Abrams' properties. There she could see one of the silver, metal boxes Otis Williams had recently placed. It had been covered with some grass and branches in an attempt to hide it from view, but she could make out the corner of the frame. I am not sure what got into her head that day; although every impulse in her bunny body must have been screaming for her to flee from the danger, Jenny decided to stop and investigate.

Cautiously she approached the box. She knew it was a trap of some kind, but she was also desperate to know how it worked. Knowledge was power, and if she could figure out the mechanics of the device, it would give everyone in the forest better odds to defeat it. As she examined the surrounding area, she noticed it was covered in a way that hid the sides and one of the ends. The other end was wide open, and it gave the impression that it was the entrance to a tunnel or some other cozy place to spend the night. Her instincts told her not to get too close to the open end, so she went around to the side and started to carefully remove some of the grass and sticks that were used to conceal it. With its camouflage slowly peeled away, Jenny could see the entire box. It had a long, rectangular shape and was made of strong, metal wire. The wire was welded in such a way that it formed evenly spaced, one-inch squares around all the sides. Inside the box she could also see a piece of meat at the far end, opposite the end that was open. A flat, slightly raised, metal plate was on the floor of the box in front of the meat. Jenny grabbed one of the sticks that had been used to hide the box and poked it through the mesh at the meat that was laying there. She flipped it over to see if it was hiding anything — a hook, or something of that nature — but by all appearances, it was just an ordinary piece of meat. She tried poking at the metal plate and as soon as she did the front of the box snapped shut with a loud bang, almost like a car door being slammed.

The sound of the door snapping closed caused Jenny to jump straight up into the air. She almost bolted back up the hill, but after a few seconds, once the burst of adrenaline had worn off and her rattled rabbit nerves had calmed down, she managed to reassure herself that she was still safe and held her ground. She looked around to see if any humans would come in response to the loud noise. When she was satisfied that no one was coming, she turned her attention back to the box. Besides, there was no way she could leave now. Her curiosity was way too intense to give up without figuring this thing out. She again approached the cage to study it further now that the trap had been sprung. Her nose twitching furiously, she approached the box slowly to continue the inspection. Now, with the door closed, she could see a wire running up from the metal plate near the meat along the side of the cage and to the front of the box. The wire was attached to what now obviously appeared to Jenny to be a latch that would release the door and close the opening. She was mad at herself for not noticing the wire in the first place before the door had slammed shut. When she had first seen it, she just thought it was part of the mesh frame. Now seeing the entrance closed off, Jenny had figured out how they would get you.

At first, you would get a whiff of a tasty snack. Your nose would lead you to what looked like a little tunnel or cavity, like a million other harmless places in the forest. There was only one way to access the food, by entering the trap through the front. The temptation would be strong for even the most cautious. You would barely even have to step inside, one quick dart in and out and the food was all yours. Without knowing it, as soon as you stepped on to the metal plate, the door would snap shut behind you and there was no way out. Jenny went over to the cage and tried pulling at the door to see if it would open again, but it was locked tight. Now she knew the humans' secret. Not only did she know the locations of the boxes, she also knew how the traps worked. Jenny knew that she had to get the word out. She had to warn everyone not to enter the boxes, no matter how hungry they were or how good the bait smelled. Jenny bounded away from the trap and headed off into the forest to sound the alarm.

CHAPTER 35

It's Not Me, Mr. Pickles

I TOOK A DEEP BREATH and slowly leaned my head around the corner again, this time risking a good, long look. Thomas and Mr. Pickles were quite distracted by each other and appeared to be unaware of my presence. Thomas was petting the cat from his head to his tail and Mr. Pickles was soaking it all in. He wove himself in and around the little boy a few times and then flopped down in front of him for some more attention. I took that as my cue to dart across the grassy opening and head for the safety of the shrubbery.

I had often wondered what it might be like to be the first penguin to jump off the ice, or the first wildebeest to wade into the rushing waters of a crocodile-filled river. Now out in the open and exposed for anyone to see — my greatest adversary and the prime suspect in a series of horrible slayings mere yards away — I ran as if my life depended upon it. I had abandoned the illusion of trying to move like a porcupine. The dainty trots and waddling motions were too slow and the risk of being seen at all was greater than the risk of someone saying, 'Hey, that porcupine moves a lot like a raccoon, could he be a raccoon in a porcupine disguise?'

Bounding across the manicured lawn, it felt good to move like myself again. After so many impressions and training sessions, I had almost forgotten how good it felt to just be a raccoon. *Why don't I just do this more often? Just be me?* As I brought my hind legs forward to make one last, giant leap into the bushes, I reminded myself what being me was actually like. The quills on my hind legs jammed into my left, front leg as it swept past. The searing pain of the quills penetrating my flesh caused my front leg to recoil, suddenly unavailable for the all-important task of balancing my body at the exact moment it when I needed it most. I went down in a tangled heap, arms and legs flailing, with my bodysuit deciding I needed an impromptu acupuncture treatment.

I crashed into the bushes but managed to bite my lip and not scream out in pain as I rolled into the underbrush. Battered and bruised — in what was essentially a fight with myself that I had somehow come out on the losing end of — I gathered my senses and checked to see if I had been discovered. To my surprise, the playful pair was still in the middle of the yard. If they had heard anything, they quickly dismissed it as the usual rustlings of the garden and went back to what they were doing.

Appreciating my good fortune in not being noticed, I then got on with the unpleasant task of pulling the quills from my flesh. As I plucked the painful protrusions, I kept a watchful eye on Thomas and Mr. Pickles. The more I observed of the boy and his dealings with the cat, the more unlikely it seemed that he could have had anything to do with the deaths of the chickens, let alone the ducks and the possums.

The quills removed and my front leg throbbing, I continued shuffling along under the cover of the bushes and along the back fence. I felt reasonably confident that unless someone was looking at the garden, intently trying to see if anyone was rustling about, I would blend in enough to make it back through the plants unnoticed. The worst part of my journey was over, at least that's what I thought.

I had almost made it back to the exit point and had just one more open area to cross to make my escape. I needed to leave the cover of the ornamental grasses, briefly expose myself in the gap, dash over to a clump of weigela bushes, and then disappear through the fence. In preparation for my final sprint, my eyes were intently fixed on Thomas, waiting for the precise moment he would turn and look back towards the house or be otherwise distracted. With all my attention focused on the boy, it took me a few seconds to realize that Mr. Pickles was . . . gone. *Where had that darn cat gotten off to?* I scanned the yard but did not see him. My mind started to race. *Now what do I do?* Less than twenty feet to go to and I would be out of the yard. The gap in the plants couldn't be more than five or six feet wide. I could just run across, and even if the boy were to see me, by the time he went and got his parents I would be long gone. Even if he were to run over to me, I would make it out through the fence before he even got close. It would expose the hidden entrance and compromise its future use, but that was a chance I had to take. I took a deep breath and darted for the exit. I thought I was home free when, who should be standing in front of me, blocking my escape but a large, angry, grey house cat.

Mr. Pickles had been sniffing at the air, when he had caught the scent of something familiar and that brought him into the bushes to investigate. Maybe he remembered me from some of our other encounters. While I was expecting the long-anticipated raccoon-on-cat battle to finally become a reality, he clearly did not expect to see a large adult porcupine come crashing to within just a few feet of him. If he had been ready to pounce, the sight of me in my disguise quickly changed his mind and he slowly began retreating. Remembering how I looked and realizing that I had the upper hand, I started walking slowly toward the big cat. He arched his back and let out a growl in order to seem as ferocious as he possibly could, but continued backing up nevertheless. Soon he had retreated past the broken fence board and I found myself standing right in front of my exit. *Goodbye, my confused friend!* I faked a final dash at Mr. Pickles, trying to convince him of his imminent impalement. As he turned tail and ran, I slipped between the broken fence boards. *Jenny was right. No one wants to mess with a porcupine.*

CHAPTER 36

Mistaken Identity

DURING JENNY'S SEARCH FOR MAX, she spread the word about the metal boxes to everyone she encountered, imploring them to resist at all costs the temptation of an easy meal. She even managed to jot down a rough map of the area, with Xs to mark the locations where she had seen the humans place the boxes. On the back of the map, she sketched a picture of how the boxes worked and a warning about the bait inside. She then passed on the map and a detailed explanation of the humans' scheme to a trusted squirrel friend, with instructions to find Max and Jonathan as quickly as squirrelly possible, without stopping to talk to anyone along the way. Among the treetops, a squirrel could almost fly — laughing at gravity as it leapt from branch to branch and tree to tree — and would surely get the message to Max faster than she could. Satisfied that she had informed enough animals herself, Jenny was confident that word of mouth had enough momentum to spread the alert to the all in the forest. She headed back to the agreed-upon rendezvous point to wait for Gary's return. When she arrived, the sun had already slipped below the horizon, and the light was fading fast.

Jenny noted to herself that the next time they needed to meet, they should not pick such a creepy location. Broken and rusted farm equipment with protruding, jagged pieces had sunk into the soft soil, and now appeared to be emerging from the ground all around her. Jenny thought to herself that the bent and twisted metal looked like the mighty claws of some long-dead beast, left to rot among the overgrown grass and weeds. The exaggerated shadows they cast in the fading light seemed like fingers reaching out from the impending darkness, intent on grasping anyone they could touch, to pull them down with them into the bowels of the earth.

The shadows grew longer and longer until they finally swallowed up what was left of the twilight, enveloping the area in darkness. The wind was picking up and the rumblings of the coming storm could be heard off in the distance. Jenny's nose twitched as she smelled the breeze, and she knew the rain was not far off. She wove her way among the twisted remains of the great metal machines until she found a location where she felt safe to observe anyone who might be coming from the direction of the Williams' place.

She tucked herself behind the front wheel of an old, abandoned tractor and hunkered down, regretting they had not chosen her comfy home as their rendezvous point. From time to time the wind would whip up and she could feel a chill as it ruffled the fur on her back. A shiver spread through her body and she was unsure if it was from the wind or the unnerving feeling she was getting from the eerie, metallic graveyard. Occasionally a gust would be strong enough that even parts of the tractor would shake a little, and the erratic clattering of metal on metal was doing little to settle her nerves.

As Jenny continued to wait behind the tractor wheel, it was getting more and more difficult to see anyone who might be approaching. She would catch movement out of the corner of her eye and thinking it might be Gary would get ready to spring from her hiding place to greet him, only to be disappointed. It would just be the swaying of the grass or something else being blown around by the approaching tempest. Her eyes were growing weary squinting into the distance when she noticed a figure finally approaching in the dark. Not wanting to get her hopes up again, she stayed huddled down until she could get a better look at who or what it was. As she anxiously waited, she could see what looked like the silhouette of a raccoon emerging from the tall grasses. *Surely that is Gary. He looks a little bigger than normal but that must just be the disguise.* When Jenny was convinced, she bounded out from her hiding place and called out to her friend, her voice piercing the night air.

Upon hearing Jenny's voice, the figure altered its course and headed directly for her. Excited to tell him everything she had learned about the boxes and how they worked, Jenny's thoughts were focused on the day's events and not on the approaching figure's identity. Only after it was too late did she realize she had made a terrible mistake.

CHAPTER 37

A Scream

As I SLIPPED OUT THROUGH the fence and disappeared up and into the undergrowth of the hillside, something was bothering me. Thomas Jackson was not at all what I had expected. It was clear that he and Mr. Pickles were good friends, and that this was not the first time they had interacted with each other. From everything Max and Jonathan had told us about the killings — those in the forest and at the ones at the Williams' place — the killer was remorseless and brutal. If it were the boy, could he be so vicious in one moment and then so tender in another, the way I just witnessed he had been with the neighborhood cat? Why spare, not just spare, but actively lavish affection upon this one creature? No, it just did not add up. The more I thought about it the surer I was that the Jackson boy could be removed from my list of possible suspects. The sun had set but I still had a little time before I had to meet Jenny. I wanted to take a look around Otis' chicken coop. In particular, I wanted to examine the child's handprint that had led Max to implicate little Thomas Jackson.

I made my way under the old barbed wire fence and into the Williams' yard. It was so much easier to get through a fence designed for cows and sheep than the newer ones that were made to be a solid wall surrounding and protecting the humans' fortresses, disconnecting them from all living things around them. If good fences make good neighbors, it means a good neighbor is someone you must not want to have any contact with.

I arrived at the chicken coop and started looking around. The feathers had been cleaned up and the ground neatly raked, but the smell of death still lingered in the air. Otis had not bothered to close the door, I guess he didn't see much point to it now. I scampered up the ramp to find the handprint Max had described to us. Fortunately, between the twilight and the light from the Williams' home I could still see enough to get a good look around. I saw the metal cage that we had watched Otis put inside the chicken coop. Normally the smell of the meat would have enticed me, but I was still full from my investigation of the Jacksons' trash. Plus, my gut was telling me to say as far away from that thing as I possibly could.

I examined the frame of the door looking for the bloody handprint. When I finally found it, my heart sank. Although it was small and the fingers childlike, I could immediately see it did not belong to a young human. The size was right, but the fingers were too narrow. The absence of any sort of thumb print just confirmed what I was thinking. I knew exactly who was behind the murders and to whom the print belonged, because this handprint was my handprint. Well, not mine specifically but the handprint of a raccoon. To confirm my theory, I found a nail that had been poking through the siding of the chicken house. I pressed the palm of my hand against it until it pierced the skin. Little drops of blood oozed out and I rubbed them over the surface of my upturned hand and fingers. Below the location of the first print, I squeezed the frame of the door, in the same manner the killer must have. When I released my hand, I had created an almost perfect replica of the original, only smaller and a little clearer. I now knew without a doubt that the killer of the chickens, and almost certainly the one behind the other murders, was a raccoon like me. It was at that very moment I heard a bloodcurdling scream off in the distance, coming from the direction of Mrs. Abrams' place.

CHAPTER 38
My Worst Fears Realized

As soon as I heard the scream, I knew something was horribly wrong. I ran as fast as I could in the direction of the danger but feared it would already be too late when I arrived. As I ran, the long grass kept hitting me in the face, scratching at my eyes and nose, accompanied by the occasional jab from my relentless quills. The pain barely even registered as my only thought was to get to Jenny as fast as I could. Closing the distance by half, I could still see nothing in the darkness. But a new sound filled my ears.

A guttural meowing sound could be heard coming from the same direction as the scream, followed by the chittering reply of the still unknown assailant. Someone new had joined the fight, and the hope that there was still enough time to intervene gave new life to my legs as I surged on to the battleground. The hissing and yowling coming from the distance made it clear to me that this new combatant had not been caught off guard and was ready for a fight. *Quarter of the way to go.* The two opponents were engaged in a fierce battle and the sounds of war filled the air. What I now concluded could only be a cat must have landed a direct blow, as the screech of a raccoon in pain was unmistakable. His counterattack was equally successful as the cat's yowl was easily heard throughout the forest and by the residents of Eleanor Place. That they were both in pain and inflicting injuries on each other would be clear to anyone who might have been listening. The only question was, who was getting the upper hand? *Almost there.* The fighting was fierce, and I was now close enough to see the shadowy outlines of the animals engaged in combat. The raccoon appeared to be gaining the advantage. I could see from the cat's posture that he was now in more of a defensive mode. Back arched and ears flattened, he was showing his side to his attacker making himself seem as big as possible. In a low growl, he tried to communicate that he was still as dangerous and ferocious as ever. The fact that he was limping and only putting his weight on three of his legs, made it clear that he was bluffing, even to me. And that meant he was in big trouble. If I could see it at my distance, his assailant must have known that the momentum of the battle had swung in his favor. Seeing that the feline was now unable to use his superior speed and agility, the aggressor's posture changed to showed that he could sense imminent victory. The attacking raccoon slowly approached his victim and backed the cat up until he came against the exterior of the stone wall that surrounded Mrs. Abrams' garden on the other side. Trapped and scared, the cat hissed and spat for all he was worth, but the situation looked hopeless. Looking to strike the final decisive blow, the menacing figure picked up a large rock off the ground and raised himself in the air on his hind legs to tower above the cowering cat. I was close enough now that I could see that he was an unusually large raccoon, much larger than me. He held the rock above his head and was preparing to smash it down upon his enemy.

The sound of me barreling across the grass caused the other raccoon to momentarily halt his attack and to turn and look in my direction. Shielded from view by the aging farm equipment, my approach could be heard by the assailant, but not seen. When I burst upon the scene he was poised to attack, the rock still menacingly brandished above his head. I threw the full weight of my body and all of my rage against him in an attempt to knock him down to the ground, and we both went tumbling into the grass and crashed against the stone wall, inches from where the cat was still crouched, awaiting his demise. As I made impact, the stone he was holding flew from his hands and hit the ground with a resonating thud. By extending his arms above his head, he had revealed his soft underbelly, and as I dove into him the quills that were on my forearms and head were driven into the side of his midsection. As we rolled and crashed into the wall, more and more quills from my bodysuit found their way into his unprotected flesh. He let out a scream and rose to defend himself, with many of the sharp shafts now protruding from multiple locations on his body. I tried to quickly return to my feet bracing for his next attack.

However, the battle with the cat, and now the jabs of my quills were more than the attacker had bargained for. Injured and in pain, he was not prepared to battle the two of us. As I gathered myself to my feet, the raucous raccoon turned and ran off into the tall grass, choosing to flee rather than continue the fight. My one good look at him was just of his backside as he disappeared into the vegetation. I stood there tense and ready for anything, afraid he would just circle around and return from another direction to launch a new attack. It was not until the sound of the assailant running through the grass grew further and further away in the distance that I was able to relax and lower my guard.

My thoughts turned to Jenny and my newfound ally. I ran over to the cat to see if he needed help and if he knew where Jenny was. As I approached, I could see the cat was Mr. Pickles. After our confrontation in the Jacksons' yard, he must have headed back home, only to stumble upon the other raccoon as he was attacking Jenny. He laid on his side against the old stone wall, bloodied and battered, ears still flat against his head as he assessed the threat of the new arrival. As I approached, he lifted his head and gave me a look of recognition, as if to say, 'You? How could it be you?' But he was too wounded and in too much agony to care. I helped him get back on his feet and nodded toward the red brick farmhouse. Understanding my intent, he allowed me to help him get on his paws again and I assisted him all the way back to the cat flap that offered warmth and safety.

As we arrived at the door, I asked Mr. Pickles if he had any idea what had happened to Jenny and where she might be. "I am not sure if she is still alive or not, but the last I saw of her, she was trying to crawl under the old tractor for safety. The big raccoon had done a number on her and he had his mouth around her neck when I confronted him. He threw her to the ground to turn and attack me. She was trying to crawl away when I engaged him, but she was in pretty rough shape."

I held the cat door open for him, to make it easier for him to get inside. I had a newfound respect for the creature that might have saved Jenny's life. It is funny how someone you think of as an adversary can become your ally. And it all started with each of us doing an unselfish act. "Thank you," I said as he slipped back into the safety of the house.

"I hope you find her," he replied as his tail disappeared. I let the door go, and as I turned to search for Jenny, I could hear it flapping back and forth behind me.

CHAPTER 39

Jenny

I FOUND JENNY UNDER THE tractor just as Mr. Pickles had said. I feared the worst as she laid there motionless, seemingly unaware of my presence even with the noise of my approach. Witnessing the ferocity of the attacks against Mr. Pickles, who at least had claws and a predator's teeth with which to try and defend himself, I knew that my sweet, soft Jenny would not have been able to mount any sort of defense. A bunny like her had so many admirable qualities: intelligence, speed, even the ability to blend into her surroundings. But none of those would be of much use when confronted and cornered by a homicidal raccoon.

She had tucked herself up against the rusted wheel of the tractor, in a final desperate attempt to find refuge, no doubt after Pickles had intervened and provided a moment of distraction. Now, as I stooped under the metal frame to retrieve my friend and companion, her blood-soaked fur offered me little hope. I could see she had been bitten and clawed in numerous places, her front, right paw had taken the worst of the damage, likely when she had raised it to defend herself.

I felt numb. I could not imagine my life without her. To think that her light which had shone so brightly could be extinguished in the blink of an eye was too much for me to bear. As I crawled under the tractor, it felt as if the whole weight of the ancient machine was on my shoulders, crushing me under its burden.

I gave Jenny's body a nudge, my heart and soul imploring her for some small movement, some sign of life. Wiping some of the blood from her face, I lowered my head and touched my nose to hers, pausing to feel the warmth of her touch for what I feared would be the last time. Nuzzling into her soft fur, head to head and nose to nose, I could feel the faintest exhalation of her breath upon my whiskers. As my eyes adjusted to the darkness under the tractor, I could see that she was still breathing. They were short, shallow, little breaths. She was alive, at least for the time being. I knew that without prompt medical attention, she would not last long.

I bit at the fabric of my bodysuit, managing to tear off both of the front legs of my outfit. Most of the quills were already gone, jabbed into my body, or into the flesh of Jenny's assailant. I carefully plucked out the last few remaining quills from the fabric and slid the elastic material over her front paw, cinching it tight and using the quills as pins to hold it in place. I hoped that the pressure of the makeshift tourniquet would be enough to slow the bleeding. There were bite marks on her neck and hindquarters, and slash marks on her face. It pained my heart to see her so broken and battered, struggling for survival. *No time to deal with that now, I will have my breakdown later. Right now, I need to get her someplace safe where she can get some help.*

It was awkward to maneuver her out from under the tractor, and I managed to gouge myself a few more times as my back scraped against the metal frame of the machine. She groaned a bit from the pain of being moved but remained unconscious. When I finally managed to get her out, I scooped her up into my arms, now bare of the porcupine disguise. Cradling her while standing on my hind legs, I started the long and arduous walk back to the forest and to the safety and help that it afforded.

It is not a natural thing for a raccoon to walk for such a long time on its hind legs. The weight of Jenny in my arms and the awkward walking position took a toll on my body. A burning sensation was spreading throughout my legs and lower back. The pain was increasing exponentially. With every fiber in my body screaming to stop and rest, I periodically looked down at my beloved friend in my arms and each time mustered up a little more strength to keep going. I negotiated with my body that if it would just go a little bit further, if I could just make it to the next tree, the next rock, then I would let it rest. I would then remorselessly break that promise and start haggling with my body all over again. The cycle repeated over and over again as I slowly made progress, one step at a time. I could not think about the destination, which, to my body, felt like an impossible task. So, I focused on what I knew I could achieve; one step at a time; one small goal after another. After what felt like an eternity, I could finally see my destination, a stately elm tree with a large mound in front of it.

"Gwendolyn!" I cried out loudly and desperately as I approached the entrance to the porcupine's home. "I need help! It's an emergency! Jenny's been hurt!"

By the time I had reached the entrance to the tunnel, Gwen was emerging from her home. "Oh, my goodness!" she exclaimed when she saw Jenny's bloodstained body. "What happened to her? Come inside, there is a spare bed that you can lay her on," she urged, as she quickly turned and headed back down into her home. Following her down the tunnel proved to be more difficult than I imagined, as I had to back myself in to make the descent as I awkwardly balanced Jenny in my arms. Lowering my head to duck down low enough to avoid the roots and the earth above me, I buried my face and mask into her blood-soaked fur. Carefully shuffling backward along the incline, I managed to carry Jenny down without incident. The sound of my yelling and all of the commotion caused all the porcupine children to gather in the living area. "Get out of the way children!" Gwendolyn barked the order with the authority only a mother could muster. As the children retreated enough to make room for me, I carried Jenny over to the little bed. There was a rush of relief in my strained body after I laid her down, as if every ounce of energy I possessed had been expended, and now my arms and legs knew they could finally rest. I immediately collapsed on to the bedroom floor in a heap, unable to move.

Gwen had already gathered bandages and brought them into the room. One of the older children soon followed with a basin of hot water and the mother porcupine began to carefully wipe the blood from Jenny's face and body. She inspected the wounds as she went and cleaned and bandaged what she could. She tore away the makeshift pressure bandage I had fashioned and rewrapped the wound on Jenny's front leg. Taking a pill from the bottle of antibiotics that we had brought for Emma, she managed to get Jenny to swallow a little bit of the medicine.

"She's in rough shape," Gwendolyn looked at her and for the first time that evening, she took a good look at me. I could see the confusion on her face as she tried to look past the disheveled version of a porcupine, with patches of quills missing everywhere, and exposed arms that did not appear to match the rest of my body. She was also trying to make sense of the vaguely familiar voice she had been hearing. "For now, that is about all we can do for her. We will keep her warm and well hydrated and give her more of the medicine, but now it is up to Jenny. I know she is a fighter. If anyone can make it, she can." She turned her attention back to Jenny and looked compassionately upon her injured friend. I breathed a sigh of relief, knowing I had brought her to the right place.

Starting to feel my strength returning, I thought it best if I retreated to a different location before our host's confusion over my identity turned into questions that I did not want to answer. Besides, my mind was spinning with the events of the evening and the thought of losing Jenny. I needed some time to process everything and start formulating a plan. While Gwen was distracted, busy attending to Jenny, I seized my opportunity to quietly slip out of the home and back into the forest.

CHAPTER 40

Identity Crisis

NOT KNOWING WHERE ELSE TO go, I headed for Jenny's place. It was close by, and from there maybe I could figure out what to do next. As I opened the door to her home, the smells and memories overwhelmed me, and I immediately felt the emptiness of her absence. The image of her, broken and bleeding in my arms, flashed into my mind and I struggled with my disquieting thoughts. My world had been turned upside down in the blink of an eye, and I had no idea what to do next, or if I even had the strength to do it alone. In one moment, I was filled with despair and loss, and in the next moment, a wave of rage and a need for revenge washed over me as my thoughts turned to the animal that had done this to her.

I made my way into the bathroom and stood in front of the mirror, the same mirror that we had stared into many times, laughing at my newfound faces. I now looked into it and could hardly recognize the face looking back at me. My dyed fur was matted with dirt and blood; my disguise was tattered and ragged. The innocence and fun of what we were doing had been unforgivingly met by the consequences of our involvement.

I turned the knobs on the faucet and let the water wash the blood off my hands. For some reason, the sound of the water was comforting, so

I let it run even as I removed the grey mask and what remained of my suit of quills. As I removed the mask that was soaked in Jenny's blood, a few drops dripped down on to the white porcelain sink. I stood there, my eyes transfixed on the mask, staring at it for the longest time. The only thing I could hear was the constant sound of the water rushing into the sink. One thought kept repeating in my mind. *How did it come to this?*

CHAPTER 41

United We Stand

THE INFORMATION THAT JENNY HAD shared with the forest creatures had spread like wildfire. Soon all the animals were made aware of the danger posed by the metal boxes and were warned to avoid the allurement of the tasty treats inside. Using the crude map that Jenny had sent with the squirrel, Max and Jonathan were able to create additional copies showing all the boxes' locations. Soon those copies were distributed throughout the forest, along with instructions that if anyone saw the humans moving the boxes, they were to follow them from a safe distance and then provide an update of the new position. In the course of one night, everyone was aware of the dangers, their locations, and how to avoid them.

Max sent out this additional message along with the maps:

> 'The only thing they are using against us is our hunger. As long as we share what we have so that no one is desperate enough to succumb to the temptation of the meat inside the traps, we can all be safe. As long as we are not focused solely on our individual benefits and wants, this plot that has been formed against us cannot succeed. Together we have learned the humans' plans. Together we can resist the humans' lures. Together we are all safe.'

Jenny was a hero, the savior of the entire forest.

CHAPTER 42

Hero

I STOOD IN FRONT OF that mirror in the bathroom for the longest time. The drops of blood from my mask had slowly streaked down the side of the sink, and when I finally broke my gaze off of the mask, I let it fall from my hands to the bottom of the basin. A new flicker of energy started to form inside of me as my thoughts cleared and I raised my head to meet the eyes of my reflection. *Lives are hanging in the balance and the perpetrator of all of this carnage is still at large.* I knew it was just a matter of time before he would return, and when he did, more souls would be lost. Someone had to stop him, and I knew that someone was me. My best chance would be to act quickly before he disappeared completely, and while he was still injured or at least weakened from the events earlier that evening.

Staring into that mirror I eventually found my strength. *This is who I am. This is who I know I want to be.* That night I made my choice. I would do what no one else could do. I would use my skills to help the ones that I love. I would protect those who cannot protect themselves, even though they might never know of the sacrifices I was about to make.

Seeing the resolve in my eyes in the image in the mirror, I knew it was time to get to work. The water still running, I reached down and splashed it on my face as I started to wash. As I cleansed myself with that water, it was as if I was washing away my old self. I felt renewed, reborn. And I was already preparing in my mind for the coming conflict.

The whiteboard was still up, and I studied it to devise my plan of action. "The attacker fled in this direction." I was not sure who I was speaking to, but the noise was better than the silence and had an added benefit — it seemed to help me think. It made me feel like Jenny was still there in the room listening to me. I used a red marker to draw an arrow indicating the assailant's last known trajectory. "That puts him on the path to the houses on the east side of the street, around Mrs. Abrams' place and towards the Asters' and Sampsons' homes, or to points beyond. "I could try the terrier costume. I know that would get me into the Asters'." On the whiteboard, I drew a little dog in the back yard of the Asters' home. I knew that the dog costume worked but it would be of little help at the Sampsons'. Plus, I had already searched the Asters' home and saw nothing that was even remotely connected to the villain I was after. That left the Sampsons' place. Of all the houses on the street, it was probably the one I knew the least about. I closed my eyes to remember as many of the details as I could. While it was true that I did not know much, I did remember one thing: the family had a large black cat.

A plan was rapidly forming in my mind. It would take a complete dye job to turn me into the Sampsons' cat. It would be messy, but at least it was fast. I grabbed the black dye and ran into the bathroom. Jumping into the bathtub, I began squirting the entire contents of the bottle on to my fur. When the bottle ran out, I started vigorously rubbing it into all my nooks and especially my crannies, until every last inch of me had been converted to black. To get at the places I could not easily reach, I laid on my back in the tub and rolled around in the inky dye that had pooled on the bottom. My mind was still thinking about what I would do if I needed to access the Asters'. No chance of transforming into Mitzy or Lulu now. I stood there in the tub, waiting for the dye to set. *What was it that Jenny said? Two animals that could go anywhere.* Then I remembered. The one big advantage of being a large, black cat is that I could transform almost instantly into a nice, smelly skunk. I just needed to be able to quickly add some white stripes.

The plan in place and the black dye set, I stepped out of the tub and toweled off a bit. Looking back at the mess I made, I knew Jenny would never let me hear the end of it if she ever saw what I had done to her bathroom. At least for that to happen she would have to be well enough to scold me, and I would just smile at every angry word coming out of her mouth. There was no time for cleaning. I had a killer to catch. I grabbed a small bottle of white dye just in case I needed it and ran off to confront an unknown enemy.

Doubts

RUNNING THROUGH THE FOREST THAT night I knew my plan still needed some work. I could easily access the yards and the houses, but I had no guarantee that the killer would be anywhere near them. Still, it did make sense. If he had been living in the ravine or anywhere else in the forest, would not some animal have seen his comings and goings, or noticed a smear of blood or some shred of evidence around his home? No, there was only one place that would make a perfect hideout if you wanted to go unnoticed and unseen, and that was in and around the homes of the humans. If I wanted to hide out of sight, that is where I would go. So, it was a reasonable assumption that this is where the rapacious raccoon must be residing.

The other problem that crossed my mind was that, even if I did find him, what would I do next? From our last encounter, it was obvious that he was larger and stronger than me. It was only the element of surprise and my unlikely ally that gave me the upper hand in our recent encounter — that and a hide full of quills. Maybe the battle had weakened him a little, but at best that might put us on equal terms. He also clearly had an advantage over me when it came to inflicting savage violence and brutality. *I just might be heroically charging into the teeth and claws that bring about my own demise.*

I tried to shake those thoughts out of my head and focus on the goal. I could not let anyone else become a victim. *One way or another, this has to end tonight.* If needed, maybe I could call on the other animals to come to my defense, or maybe I could find a way to get the humans to help. No plan is ever foolproof. Waiting for the perfect moment often just leads to inaction. Sometimes you just have to take a leap and make the rest up as you go along.

As I pressed on, I reached the edge of the forest and the lights from Mrs. Abrams' place came into view. The night was getting darker and the stars were no longer visible in the sky. The wind was whipping up even more than before and the smell of rain was in the air. Without a doubt a storm was coming soon. I lowered my head and summoned my tired legs to continue pressing forward. Despite all my doubts, there was one thing I was absolutely sure of: it is much easier to run disguised as a cat than as a porcupine.

CHAPTER 44

Confrontation

I KEPT RUNNING UNTIL I had passed the Asters' place and came to the spot where the two properties met. The fence at the Sampsons' was a low, chain-link type and would be easy to climb over. Gripping the links in the fence, I caught my breath for a minute and then took a moment to survey the yard. It was well illuminated by the light emanating from inside the house. I scanned for any signs that the other raccoon was nearby. There were a myriad hiding places he could have used as cover. Still clinging to a large tree was a neglected fort that the children had used when they were little. Playground equipment that had not been touched by a child in a decade sat rusting, seemingly frozen in time. A shed and some other small structures were scattered around the property, as well as what appeared to be an automobile under a blue tarp in the far corner. With so many hiding places, I realized he could be almost anywhere.

I closed my eyes and tried to settle my mind and engage my other senses, drawing deep breaths through my nostrils to inhale the scent of my surroundings. I was not sure how, but as I drew in the moist night air, I knew that he was present. I could sense it. With my eyes still closed, I leaned my head a little toward the house and listened as intently as I could. Even in what appeared to be a quiet night, I could hear a cacophony of noise; the sound of a car in the distance — *eliminate that*; some mechanical sounds, maybe fans running — *eliminate that*. I kept listening until I had filtered out every irrelevant sound and all other extraneous data. With all of those noises dismissed, I focused in on the one thing that sounded like a clue. I could hear a very faint scratching sound coming from the roof. Someone was moving along the top of the Sampsons' house.

I stealthily slunk over the fence and made my way across the grass. My eyes were focused on the roof, looking for any kind of movement against its black surface. As I approached, I could make out the outline of an animal crawling down the slanted rooftop. He was heading towards an open window on the second floor.

When I got to within a few feet of the house, I could see what he was doing. A large drainpipe ran down from the roof gutter, past the open window, and down to the ground. The prowling raccoon used the pipe to climb down to the windowsill, tore open the window screen in one quick swipe of his paw, and stood there peering into the house. "Stop!" I cried out. "What are you doing?"

The other raccoon turned his head and squinted through the darkness trying to see me. Even with the light from the house, he couldn't locate the source of my voice; one advantage of being dyed all black on a stormy night. "I am putting an end to it all," he called out into the gloom from his stage up on the ledge. "I am putting an end to these humans. I am putting an end to the animals in the forest. We were not meant to live like this, so close to the humans. They have destroyed our homes and our families. The animals are just as guilty. In the hope of an easy meal, they have become complicit with these humans. They eat their trash and lick the liquids from their bottles. They do nothing to defend themselves or the purity of their forest homes. I am going to see to it that no peace will ever exist between us and them. I will destroy what they love so that they will have no choice but to respond in kind." With that, he turned away and entered the house through the newly torn screen. As he disappeared into the house, I could hear the faint sound of a baby's giggle.

CHAPTER 45

All Alone

THE WIND HAD BEEN PICKING up as the night went on. Distant sounds of thunder were rolling ever closer. On the horizon, a few flashes of lightning lit up the night sky, signaling the coming of the rain. The storm was rolling in from the east and the Sampsons' back yard was a great place to watch the lightning. It was at that fateful moment that John and Elizabeth Sampson had decided to go outside on a warm, summer evening to watch the show. With the baby asleep upstairs in her crib and the older children away, they would have some quiet time to themselves. If only they would have turned back and looked at the house, they would have seen what appeared to be the family cat frantically climbing up a drainpipe to get to the open, second floor window.

CHAPTER 46

The Battle Within

I THOUGHT FOR SURE I would be too late when I finally made it up the pipe and onto the window ledge. The masked intruder had a good head start on me and I feared that I was about to cast my eyes upon a scene that would make the carnage from the chicken coop seem like child's play. From the window sill, I passed through the ripped screen and onto a changing table in front of the window. It was difficult to see, the only light coming from the dim orange glow of a nightlight plugged into the wall across from me, but it provided enough illumination that I could make out the rough details of the baby's room. To my right, I could see the child's crib in the corner of the room. Shelves full of books and wide-eyed stuffed animals ran along the walls above where the baby slept. Across from the window near the nightlight, there was a rocking chair with a yellow cushion next to a pink dresser, decorated with various stickers of cute, little forest critters. *Boy did they get it wrong. Where is the sticker depicting a deranged, murderous raccoon?* A tall lamp was to my left, as well as a chest overflowing with toys. To my relief, the infant appeared fine for now, and I could hear the happy cooing sounds a baby makes coming from the crib. She was unaware that she was in any danger, just doing what babies do. Cautiously, and as quietly as I could, I moved to the end of the changing table and scanned intently around the room for the intruder.

A sudden flash of lightning came to my aid and bathed the room in its bright light, and —for a brief instant — I could see as clear as day a large raccoon standing on his hind legs holding on to one of the crib's spindles with his paw. And in his other hand, he held a large pair of scissors. There is a period of calm between a flash of lightning and the anticipated boom of the thunder, and in the moment in between, the menacing raccoon asked: "Do you think you can stop me from harming this child?" He did not take his eyes off the baby as he spoke, his voice solemn and devoid of emotion. The thunder then clapped emphatically like some kind of ominous applause before he spoke again in his dreadful tone. "No one can save her. She has no future. If you try and stop me, I will only destroy you as well. Turn around and leave. You might as well save yourself." He finally broke his gaze off the baby and glared at me with his piercing, black eyes.

"Why would you do this horrible thing? If you think I will just leave so you can murder this innocent child, you are crazier than I thought." I tried to keep my voice brave, but a slight quiver could be detected as I finished my sentence. This might have been the biggest, meanest looking raccoon I had ever seen. He let go of the crib and started moving towards the changing table, still brandishing the scissors. *How does one keep from being stabbed with a pair of scissors?* I tried to stall for time. "You said that this would be the end of it all. How does attacking this baby end anything? What are you trying to accomplish?" I was hoping my questions would slow his approach as I frantically looked around for anything I could use to defend myself. Finding a small blanket folded on the corner of the changing table, I unfolded it and placed it on to my shoulders in case he lunged at me with the scissors. My thinking was that if he came at me, using the scissor blades like a knife, I could then swirl the blanket around and try to smother the sharp point, instead of allowing it to plunge unabated into my flesh. Or it might sheathe the tip just enough so as to minimize any damage and leave me still capable of a counterattack. At least that was the plan. I tied the two corners of the blanket around my neck so that it would stay on my back and not fall to the floor when I needed it the most. It also had the added benefit of allowing me to keep my hands free for the impending fight.

"When the humans find the baby dead, in their shock and outrage they will destroy the forest. They will drive out or kill every animal for miles. The animals will have no choice but to flee from this place and never return. The ones that survive will have to live like animals are supposed to live, wild and free, with no contact with the humans, as nature intended it to be. The animals already blame the humans for the recent killings in the forest. They will be so traumatized by this new onslaught they will teach generations of their young to avoid human contact at all costs. It will come at the sacrifice of many lives, but the animals will be happy again. And their families will live in peace. The balance of nature will be restored." There was a cold detachment in his voice as he spoke. There was also something familiar that I just could not place. Another crack of lightning and a few seconds later, the roar of thunder filled the night air.

"You will cause the deaths of hundreds of souls and destroy countless lives," I said as I backed away from the edge of the changing table. The massive raccoon had reached the base and started to climb up onto the far end of the table as I spoke. The curtains on either side of the window were reaching into the room as the wind from the open window had caused them to come to life. "You do not need to do this. We can have happy lives just the way things are. The animals in the forest can adapt to being near the humans. There is no reason to take such extreme action. Think about your family. Would your father want you to be doing this?" I thought that maybe if I could reach his heart, and prick his conscience, I could stop all of this without a fight. It was to no avail as he just kept slowly advancing towards me, twirling the scissors in his hand like he was a gunslinger from the old west.

"My father was a no-good glutton and drunk who destroyed our family. And where do you think he got the food and booze from?"

Well, so much for appealing to his sentimental side. I should get this guy to meet my father. We might have a lot in common. That is when it hit me. *I think this guy does know my father.* "Derek?" I asked cautiously. The question caught the advancing aggressor off guard, and for the first time, he seemed a bit taken back.

"How do you know my name you mangy cat?" In his confused state, he halted his approach and lowered the scissors.

I had forgotten what I must have looked like from his point of view and tried to seize the opportunity it presented. "I know that name because it is my brother's name."

"That's impossible. How could you be my brother?" At least he was confused instead of angry.

"You are my brother . . . because I am Gary." I adjusted my posture to appear less catlike.

He stared at me through the dim light, trying to make sense of our conversation. "Gary? Is that you? You look so different. It has been so long . . . but it doesn't matter now. It's too late. I have already killed so many, and now I must bring my plan to its conclusion. I will give you one last chance brother. Go! Now! Take whatever friends or family you might have and get as far away from this place as you can. This is your last chance!" I could see his grip on the scissors tightening again.

"Listen to me, Derek. You are trying to convince me that the humans were the cause of your unhappy family. It is true that being near them might have made it easier for our father to get the food and alcohol that he destroyed himself with, but he chose to do those things. He could have stopped. He could have quit drinking and could have been kind to you and me and mom. He made his decisions and he was the one that put them into action, and you are right, we suffered the consequences. So did he. You killing this child will not change any of that. Right now, you have the same choice he did. Whatever bad you have done in the past, you have the choice now, at this moment, to do something good. To make the right decision and change from this path that you are on. Whatever you are feeling, whatever your emotions are telling you to do, or whatever vengeance you are trying to exact for the abuses unjustly inflicted upon you, it all can change with the next choice you make tonight. It all starts with this first decision to do what is good because you know deep down inside that is what you should do. You can make the choice you wish our father had made all those years ago. Walk away from this and you can disappear from this place and start your life over again."

I braced myself for an attack. I thought I sounded convincing, but I could see the emotion and rage building in him. "You think it is that easy?" Derek seethed with anger and hate. "He destroyed my life!" He moved into an attack stance, raising the scissors in front of him again.

"Did *he* destroy your life? He is not here with you now. He is not the one about to murder his brother and a defenseless infant. You and I grew up in the same house with the same father and mother. I made a choice to be here tonight to do the right thing, to protect others and stand up for justice. I am now choosing to risk my life to save this innocent human child. With all the same influences that you had, I am choosing to be good, and to put the needs of others ahead of my own. You want to blame someone for destroying your life? Why don't you blame yourself? You made the same kinds of choices and mistakes you are hating our father for. You are blaming everything and everyone else for your problems as if that is some kind of excuse for you to do anything you want to, to indulge any angry thought or to give free rein to any negative emotion as if that is a justifiable reason to lash out at others. The only one you have to blame is yourself!"

With that Derek let out a loud howl and charged towards me, scissors raised above his head, ready to be plunged into my body. I spun the blanket from around my neck, to envelop the scissors. Engulfed in the fabric, the blow from the scissors glanced off my belly and did not pierce my skin as Derek had intended. I countered his attack by using his own forward momentum to push him off the end of the changing table. He hit the floor with a resounding thud, crashing into the lamp and shattering the glass in the process. Springing back to his feet, he leaped back up on the table and locked into battle, teeth bared and claws ready for gouging. All the noise and commotion woke the baby from its slumber, and now confused and frightened, she started to cry for her mother, loud enough that even with the noise from the wind of the approaching storm, her parents could hear her outside through the open window.

John and Elizabeth had still been in the yard watching the night sky when the baby started crying. Out of instinct they both turned and looked up, only to see in the window of their baby's bedroom two dark figures standing on the changing table, fighting and clawing each other. Another flash of lightning revealed the true nature of the scene. A large and sinister looking raccoon was engaged in a fierce battle with the family cat, who for some reason was wearing a cape.

Elizabeth screamed while John sprinted to the back door to rush up to the baby's room. He was halfway up the stairs when the final blow of the fight was delivered. Distracted by the scream, Derek looked out at the hysterical woman in the yard below. In his hesitation, I threw my shoulder and all my weight into his midsection and pushed him out the window. Caught unaware by my sudden charge, he was unable to brace himself to absorb the impact of my blow. His hands reached and grasped at the window frame in a desperate attempt to keep his balance, but his momentum was too great. He stumbled backward off the ledge and disappeared from my sight.

In my desperate attempt to save both myself and the baby, I had thrown all of my weight with full force in order to push my bigger brother out the opening with little thought as to how to stop my own forward velocity. Reaching out reflexively, I scraped my claws across the wooden window frame, frantically trying to get a pawhold. When they finally dug in and I regained my balance, a hot surge of electricity ran through my entire body, relieved that I had not precipitously suffered the same fate as my brother.

I peered over the ledge of the windowsill, half expecting to see Derek's broken body splayed out on the ground below. *No way he could have survived that. Not being so off balance when he fell.* To my shock, when I looked down, I could saw him standing there, seemingly unharmed. He shook himself off and looked up at me perched upon the sill; both of us staring at each other, trying to figure out what to do next. From the sound of John Sampson's footfalls, I realized he had reached the top of the stairs, and I knew I only had a couple of seconds before he would burst into the room. I couldn't stay, and I did not want to gamble that I could survive the jump to the ground. One misplaced chair or metal stake pointing up at me and I would be done for. Even with a good landing, a hurt or broken leg would mean Derek could quickly finish what he started.

The only way out was up. So, I scrambled up the drainpipe and on to the roof with the blanket still tied around my neck. Derek's only direct path out of the yard was blocked by the still shrieking Elizabeth Sampson. Seizing his chance to escape, he bolted towards the fence between the two homes, and as he ran, I could see that he was limping. *The fall must have done some damage after all.* Knowing that I could not let him escape into the night, only to pursue his agenda again once he had healed, I started my pursuit of him along the roof, running in parallel with him along the length of the house.

While Derek was struggling to get himself over the fence and into the Asters' yard, I was facing another problem; I was running out of roof to run on. The approaching storm was intensifying, and the flashes of lightning would frequently brighten the sky, its electricity streaking through the air. With the night light up, I could see that there was a large maple tree, in the Asters' yard, with a branch that had grown over the fence and had snaked out to within a few feet of the roof's edge. With all the adrenaline surging through my body, I didn't even slow down as I approached the edge of the building. With one glorious leap, I jumped off the roof and on to the tree branch, scrambling down the tree to the Asters' yard below.

Before I made it to the ground, Derek had climbed over the fence and was hobbling across the yard, heading to the back corner of the Asters' garden. I wondered to myself if he was aware of the escape route under the fence that the terriers had dug out. Based on my earlier experience at the Asters' home, a plan was formulating in my mind. I knew that if I ran near the patio area, I could trigger the automatic lights and knock over a chair or anything on hand that would create noise. With the lights on and a commotion in the yard, Mitzy and Lulu would surely take notice of the intrusion and come barreling out through the pet door. With Derek injured and limping, I should be able to overtake him and find a way to impede his progress, just enough so that the dogs could catch him. At that point I would not have to outrun the terriers; they would attack the first raccoon they could reach. All I had to do was stay ahead of Derek.

I swerved from my pursuit and ran towards the Asters' home and the patio area outside the kitchen. The motion sensing lights awoke and illuminated the area as planned, and I leapt on to a chair and knocked it over into a planter. The resulting noise was loud as intended, and right on cue the dogs start barking furiously inside the house. It would be a matter of just a few seconds before they would come pouring into the yard. I resumed my pursuit of Derek who by now had made it across most of the yard and was nearing the corner garden with the escape tunnel.

I may have miscalculated. With Derek just a few feet from safety, the sound of the crazed terriers entering the yard caused me to wonder about the saneness of my plan. It was becoming apparent to me that not only was Derek able to cross the yard faster than I thought, but I also may have been a little too optimistic about the speed of my own escape. In a flash-back to a childhood memory, the tip of my tail felt a twinge of pain.

Derek had made it to the bushes, and if he had not been so distracted by the sound of the dogs, he might have noticed that the often-used egress under the fence no longer existed. Instead, something that looked like a tunnel was in its place, disguised by some branches and grass that were placed in such a way so as to conceal its true nature.

As I reached the bushes, I could hear a loud bang, like the sound of a car door being slammed shut. Arriving at the tunnel, it was clear that it had been filled in and one of the humans' metal boxes had been placed in the corner. Derek, now trapped, was seething and hissing; biting and clawing at the steel mesh that now held him inside. The barking of the terriers was drawing ever closer, and I knew I did not have long before they arrived. In the distance, I heard the patio door slide open as Claude and Julia Aster joined the scene to investigate what it was that set the dogs off. With sad-ness I looked at my brother for one last time, knowing that he was about to fall into the very hands of the humans he had blamed for all of his troubles.

I scrambled up the wooden fence that ran along the back of the yard, and from the safety of the fence top, I looked down as Mitzy and Lulu as they arrived at the metal box. Derek had defensively backed himself into the far corner and the two dogs were lunging at the cage in an attempt to play with their newfound toy. I stood upon my hind legs and reached a sympathetic paw out to my brother; one last gesture before I went over the fence and left him to whatever fate the humans had in store for him. In that instant, the heavens opened up and the rain came pouring down.

If anyone had looked up at the fence when the rain started to come down, they would have seen standing there — his cape flapping in the wind — the real hero of Eleanor Place; the one who risked his life to save others and to bring peace to the forest.

CHAPTER 47

Epilogue

THE EVENTS OF THAT STORMY night began an eventful week on the street know as Eleanor Place. The local media caught wind of the story of the daring cat that fought off a rabid raccoon (the media always has to embellish a bit) to save the life of little baby Sofia. We learned that the large black cat's name was Charlie, and while confused about all the commotion around him, in a very cat-like manner he decided to go with it, reveling in all of the attention. The story got picked up by the national news and soon his face was on televisions and newspapers across the world. Elizabeth even sewed up a little cape to match what she thought she saw that night. Of course, despite searching the yard and the street, she was never able to find the original for some strange reason. The image of Charlie wearing the cape soon went viral. He even got a lucrative deal to do a commercial — with the cape on of course. Everyone was calling him 'the cat crusader'.

With the extra income from the endorsements, the Sampson family was able to do some much-needed renovations on their home. In the course of replacing their roof, it was discovered that there was a hole in the abandoned fireplace chimney that led into the attic. It appeared that some kind of animal had been nesting in the attic for years and had done some damage to the insulation. The contractor's best guess was that it was a raccoon.

Max and Jonathan received a second or third-hand anonymous tip, possibly originating from a stray cat that was in the neighborhood, that the killer who had been prowling the forest was indeed gone. Most of the animals were still on edge for a week or two after that report broke, but with no new deaths during that time, the forest and everyone in it gradually returned to normal. Max marked his case file closed, happy that the saga was over, and that justice had been served. He was just a little bit disappointed not to have been a part of the end game. Sometimes that is just how these cases go. Maybe the next one will be different.

Otis Williams eventually gave up on his trapping program. He was in disbelief that after weeks of baiting and setting traps — even switching baits from chicken to fish and even marshmallows — besides the one raccoon, the only thing he had caught in any of the traps was Mr. Pickles, and on numerous occasions I might add. Pickles had figured out that he could gorge himself on the tasty treats inside and then all he had to do was take a little nap while he waited to be released.

Looking for closure, Otis ended up blaming the deaths of his chickens on the one raccoon that he did catch. Must have had rabies or something he figured. Claude Aster had placed the trap in his garage to keep the animal away from Mitzy and Lulu, and in a desperate attempt to quiet the dogs down. The next morning, he called animal control and a rather odd man wearing a shirt that said 'I love hairless cats' came and took the raccoon away.

Otis got himself a dozen new baby chicks, Rhode Island Reds this time; described as hardy, happy-go-lucky birds and proficient egg layers. He then set to work on beefing up the security on the coop and installing an automatic door on the hen house. Esther regularly reminded him that the hundreds and hundreds of dollars he spent could have bought all the eggs he could eat for the rest of his life and then some, but in Otis's words: "They just don't taste right!"

As for me, when I was standing on the fence that night, my cape flapping in the wind and the rain pouring down, I knew that I had found my calling. The forest was safe, and justice was served on my brother for all the things he had done. How his anger led him to go so far and to lash out at so many innocent individuals, I will never know. As a child I thought of his violence as heroic; striking out at the oppressor who was our father. Now I can see he let his hate and his need for revenge drive him to do things even our father never did. He had allowed the negative qualities of the man he resented, to shape and mold his personality and choices in life.

My childhood had had its rough moments, but there was one valuable lesson I took from all of my experiences. You cannot control what the people around you are going to do or who they are going to be, even if they are the people we love the most. They may make choices we don't agree with, and sometimes we even have to suffer the consequences of their bad decisions. But the only thing you can control is how you are going to react to those people and to the events that happen around you. My brother allowed himself to become bitter and angry, and it destroyed his life and the lives of others he came in contact with. With the same experiences, I had found a way to help others and to be proud of the things I did and the person I was.

I do know no single person can give you everything you need. I had to learn to take the good that people gave me and forgive the rest. My father was a drunkard and violent at times which is inexcusable, but I try to remember him as a man who gave me life and provided food and shelter when I was unable to do so for myself. After my father had died, my mother, with the knowledge that she was now safe, finally allowed herself to collapse under the weight of all the burdens she had been carrying. She tried her best to put on a brave face but had difficulty motivating herself to do the simplest of tasks that were needed to keep a household functioning. Her depression grew and grew until she spent most of her days in bed. Still, I was able to look past the neglect of my own emotional needs, to see a woman who sacrificed everything to try her best to save her family and care for her kids. At least that approach kept me from becoming bitter. I had learned that people are only ever going to give you so much. Maybe it is all they are capable of. Maybe it is all they choose to share. Maybe they are barely treading water themselves. Who knows? Who you want to be is always in your own hands, and in the next decision that you make.

If all of that seems a bit too rosy and unrealistic, I will be honest and share with you that I am not without scars from my experiences. I have my days when I am sad and unmotivated for no apparent reason. Some days, even when I am around the ones that I love, I feel as if I am wearing a mask. I know those periods are coming from my insecurities about myself, and my feelings of self-doubt, and I know that I am not immune to the influence that they still exert upon me in the present. Maybe that is what they mean by the expression 'no man is an island'. None of us can go unscathed or unaffected by the people around us. Even someone who physically or emotionally has removed themselves from the world around them was probably driven to that place by the experiences they shared with others.

With all of the events that transpired, I did learn that you can place two people in an almost identical situation and get two completely different results. Was it the infinitesimally small variables in the circumstance that made such a dramatic difference? Or was it a choice about how we processed those experiences? For me and my brother, it seemed to be the latter. Maybe that is my true superpower.

After I had left the street and made it back to the safety of the woods, I headed straight to Jenny's place for a long hot shower. I knew it would take multiple shampoos to see any of my original markings. It took me a couple of hours, and at times I thought all of my fur would fall out, but I managed to wash up to the point that I looked like a raccoon again, albeit somewhat muted. With that, I left to go see Jenny.

When I arrived at the porcupine den, it seemed so ominously quiet that I began to fear the worst. I called out to Gwen from the entrance of the den, "Gwendolyn? Are you home? It's me Gary — Jenny's friend. I heard she was hurt and brought to your home. Is she all right? Can I see her?" It seemed best to pretend that I knew nothing, in case in all the confusion the family did not recognize me from before, and the identity of the heroic 'porcupine' that rescued her remained a mystery. I waited for a few painstaking minutes before a light turned on and someone came to the door.

"Do you have any idea what time it is? We were all in bed! Yes, Jenny is here. Come on in." The porcupine gave an irritated wave, indicating for me to come inside and turned to go back into her home. I guess with everything that had happened I had forgotten what time it was. We headed over to the bed where I had laid Jenny, which now felt like a lifetime ago.

"How is she doing?" I could see she was sleeping peacefully and tried not to wake her up.

"She had some close calls. I cleaned up all her wounds and bandaged them the best I could, but I think the medicine I gave her might be what makes the difference. Isn't that a funny thing? The medicine that she brought to save Emma will probably end up saving her. Life is funny how things work out sometimes. She woke up briefly and was able to take a drink of water, which was a positive sign. She asked for you, where you were, and if you were okay." She turned and gently placed her paw on Jenny's head. "You are welcome to stay here with her if you like," she said with a yawn. And with that, the mother porcupine headed for her bed and left me alone with Jenny.

My body was too sore and tired to move anymore, so I sat down beside her on the floor and leaned my head against the bed. I reached over and started to gently stroke the soft fur on her face. I sat there watching her breathe — grateful that she was still alive — until the weight of my eyelids overpowered me and I fell asleep beside her.